Good

Man's

Croft

Good Man's Croft

JOHN M. BREWER

iUniverse LLC
Bloomington

Good Man's Croft

iUniverse books may be ordered through booksellers or by contacting:

iUniverse LLC
1663 Liberty Drive
Bloomington, IN 47403
www.iuniverse.com
1-800-Authors (1-800-288-4677)

ISBN: 978-1-4759-9919-8 (sc)
ISBN: 978-1-4759-9921-1 (hc)
ISBN: 978-1-4759-9920-4 (ebk)

Library of Congress Control Number: 2013913170

Printed in the United States of America

iUniverse rev. date: 07/27/2013

CONTENTS

To my " yoke mate "

ORIGINS

I sat next to my great-great-grandfather, struggling with a feeling of hopelessness: how could I get any information out of him that would be of any use? He had to be well over ninety, exactly how over I don't think anyone knew. He stared at me, his jaw moving as though he were chewing something, though I knew he had no teeth. Despite this, I could understand him well enough. I was twelve and tasked by the schoolmaster with extracting any family legend or history I could, writing it up and relating it to the other students. We all had to do this.

I asked him, "Where did our family come from?" I guessed that asking specific questions would be better.

He looked at me until I was preparing to ask him again, when he said, "From south."

"Southern England?" I asked.

More stare, then, "No. Far south." More silence before he said, "Walked a long way."

I asked, "Why did they leave?"

He at length replied, "Lost a fight. Lost their land. Settled here because only land open. Walked a long way."

I wrote down what he had said, which wasn't hard because it wasn't much, and then I inquired, "How did they cross the Channel?"

He shook his head, repeated, "Walked a long way."

This confused me: I asked again, "How did they cross the Channel?"

He looked irritated and said, "No channel then. Dry."

I wrote that down, disbelieving, yet it was a definite statement. "So our family has been here thousands of years?" I concluded. He nodded. I asked, "What does our name mean?" Our family name, Mendy, was unusual.

My ancestor replied, "Means 'hill'. We lived on a hill. South. Far south."

"In France?" I asked.

"Spain," he replied.

I wrote this all down, then wondered, "Did they farm or hunt?"

He told me, "Both. Had to pay rent. Hard life. Neighbours didn't like us. We had poorest land. High meadow. On Landrum estate now."

I wrote all this down. I knew the meadow he was talking about. There was also a patch next to the meadow, a few acres of wilderness. It seemed too small for hunting and I wondered why it wasn't farmed. Was the soil too poor? I asked, "What is the patch of wilderness next the meadow for?"

My great-great-grandfather was silent so long I thought he hadn't heard me or else had forgotten my question. However he eventually said, "That's 'good man's croft'. Left for the devil." More silence, then, "Bad place. Stay out. Children sacrificed."

I had never heard of this before, but he seemed very much in earnest. I wrote down what he had said. I couldn't think of any other questions, so went to write up what I had heard. It seemed fantastic, but I had my instructions.

A few days after, it became too late to ask him any more questions. My great-great-grandfather died in his sleep. Though I daresay I had been closer to him than anyone else in our family—I was his namesake, we were both named David Mendy—my feeling was of severed connections with the past, lost history. Since my grandfather and great-grandfather had died already, that left my father and me.

My father was also a schoolmaster, teaching in the same Council school. He didn't make much money, one reason my mother left him in 1895 when I was four. I had begun to realize my father was a disappointed man, and my mother's defection left him silent and bitter. We spoke very little; it was a silent household. Because of his profession, I had long understood I was expected to do well in school, so I worked very hard. I wasn't sure what goal or end my efforts were in aid of, perhaps teaching school myself.

* * *

My family legend stirred up some controversy. The master was disposed to be sceptical, intimating I had invented it all, but I insisted I had faithfully reported what I had been told. The other students of course followed his lead, so my efforts seemed about to be submerged in ridicule, until I got to the part about the good man's croft. Several of the students had heard of the legend or custom that part of every farmer's field was supposed to be left to an evil spirit, or the devil, or evil spirits in general. This made everyone thoughtful, though there were still a few sceptics. Several of these challenged me or each other to visit or better yet, spend the night in the good man's croft on the Landrum estate. However, the master warned everyone that what was proposed involved trespassing. So things quieted, to my relief, for my great-great-grandfather's warning had impressed me, I wasn't sure why.

* * *

3

Later that year, after end of term, my father had gone over my marks. I had expected praise, for I had done well, but, in one of our very rare conversations, he told me he expected me to do as well next year, my upper fourth. This so I might gain a scholarship to attend a grammar school about twenty miles away. He seemed unhappy as usual, but I realized his unhappiness was chronic and had nothing to do with me. I also realized he expected me to be successful, it didn't matter in what, just that I was to do better than he had. For me, that meant education.

I took his comments seriously enough so that I spent part of the summer studying, trying to gain some advantage. Otherwise, I wandered. I liked to walk, to be alone with my thoughts, a solitary wanderer. I tried to avoid the other boys; they were inclined to bully me, another reason for being alone.

Our parish was moderately hilly, gently rolling country. To the northwest of our parish, beyond Cirencester, the land rose to form the watershed that separated the tributaries of the Thames from those of the Avon. The eastern edge of our parish was defined by a small stream that ran into a larger one, an actual tributary of the Thames. I had been made aware that my presence in the eastern parish was unwelcome, for reasons I didn't understand, so I confined my rambles to my own parish.

In wet weather, unfortunately a common occurrence, I would sit at the table in the front parlour and read or pore over maps, for my father had survey maps of the area. My father didn't teach history, but was interested in the subject. If I wanted a conversation with him, I would ask about historical features of the area. I learned, for example, there was a very old road or track way called Akeman Street to our north running roughly east and west. A Roman road to our west went to Cirencester. There was a curious mound, called a "camp", north of our parish. My father thought this an ancient fortification, for the remains of walls and ditches were too large, still, to be considered a pen for cattle. I found this to be rather interesting, but in a way frustrating, for even approximate dates were wholly speculative, "prehistoric" said my father, forestalling my questions.

Much closer to the present day were the remains of tenant houses, a few still intact and occupied, including the one we lived in. My father told me our parish was farmed, supported a considerable population, until the ancestors of the Landrums had decided more money could be made raising sheep. So the tenants had to leave. I sensed my father did not approve of what must have been an enormous disruption of many lives. The fields themselves were enclosed by dry stone walls, and my father told me these were from a much older time, again "prehistoric". There were wooden gates to provide access to the fields, but these were always chained.

The field below the high meadow and good man's croft was often host to a considerable flock of sheep, sometimes with a shepherd in attendance, usually not. If there was a shepherd, I wouldn't venture to cross the dry stone wall, lest the shepherd set his dog on me. Given the reputation of the Landrum family, I thought this a real danger. If there was no shepherd, then I could cross. By now, I was big enough so the sheep made way for me; when I was small, the creatures frightened me.

* * *

I often ventured, in absence of shepherds, onto the high meadow that my distant ancestors lived on. I now regarded this as my ancestral patch next the good man's croft. On one summer day, I walked up there. I tried to lie down in the high meadow to watch the clouds casting moving shadows along the green land. However, the ground was stony, lie as I might, so I had to stand. The good man's croft as usual seemed to loom: great trees, a tangle of branches, some limbs flourishing, some broken, while the plants closer to the ground were dark as though stained by permanent shadow. All very unlike the other patches of woods round about which were much more open, the grass and other plants between the trees green and lush. This reinforced my reluctance to explore the good man's croft. I stayed clear of it.

Walking about the meadow, I eventually detected a ring of stones, about 15 feet across. The stones were only slightly above the level of the surrounding soil, so had been in the ground a long time. I kicked and scraped dirt from around two or three of the stones, working at loosening them. At length I was able to pull up two of them. They were unworked stones, one with a pointed end, otherwise quite unremarkable, a considerable disappointment. I liked to think these were the foundation of our dwelling. In the centre, once I had scraped away enough dirt, I thought I detected charcoal, the remains of perhaps millennia of fires. The good man's croft lay silent and sinister. I didn't even see any birds flying about the trees.

Finally I walked down the stony edge of the high meadow and good man's croft, across the pasture where the sheep grazed, and over the dry stone wall. I set out for my home, the summer sun blessedly warm on my shoulders. Glancing back, still no birds moved about the good man's croft.

The following day, it rained. Despite the disappointment of my essay into archaeology the day before, I perused my father's survey maps with greater interest. I looked farther afield, across the Thames, until my eye caught a location called "Liddington Castle." This stirred my imagination with images of battlements and turrets and I asked my father if there was an actual castle there. My father shook his head and said, "People often call ruins of earthworks 'castles.' This one used to be called 'Mount Badon.'" Here he put his finger on the place where a village sat at the base of the hill. I saw the name Badbury. My father continued, "This is where King Arthur stood and sent off the besieging Saxons."

"When was this?" I asked.

Unusually, my father had a fairly precise answer, "About 490 A.D. This gave the land fifty years of peace." My father was silent, and then continued, "Two of our Mendy ancestors, father and son, stood with King Arthur here. One was wounded, but both survived."

I caught a hint of something in my father's voice that I hadn't heard before. After a few seconds, I realized it was pride, pride in our ancestors' deeds. At this point, lunch was served and this ended our conversation. But I very much wanted to see the place.

The next day being dry and sunny, I left our house after breakfast and walked southeast. I crossed the Thames at Kemble, using the bridge, the first across the Thames. I turned more southwest, walking toward rising ground. Then I saw what had to be the place: a low, wide, flat-topped hill, ridged at the top with what I realized must be the remains of earthworks. The western end was steep. On top of the hill was a small cluster of fir trees, nothing else. As I mounted the hill, I crossed a flat place that extended to my left and right. Its way was marked by a path of daisies, now a little past their peak, but very striking nonetheless. I understood this must be the Ridgeway, another "prehistoric" road. To my right beyond the steep western edge of the hill, I could see a road going north-south. This had to be the Roman road, so this hill commanded a juncture of two roads, probably important roads, hence the siege.

Near the top were remains of three or four concentric ditches, once probably separated by walls, palisades of timber. I stood atop the hill looking about me. The day was clear and I could see Cirencester about 15 miles north and several villages I recognized, including my own. I tried to imagine standing here, spear in hand, awaiting the onslaught of the Saxon "shield-wall." I was stirred. This was my land, my forefathers' land, and for the first time, I felt myself worthy of my heritage, never mind how our neighbours thought of us.

I would have stayed longer enjoying this feeling of belonging, but the time lunch was served at our place was approaching, and I was hungry. So back I went, walking fast, occasionally running, at least on the downhill parts. I managed to be in time for lunch. In keeping with his custom, my father didn't ask me where I had been; and in keeping with my custom, I didn't tell him.

*   *   *

Toward end of term the following spring, I received a letter from the grammar school admitting me with a scholarship. I showed this to my father, expecting him to be pleased, to praise my efforts, display some emotion, but he only nodded.

I knew I would need money even with the scholarship. I thought and thought: what could I do to earn money? We had a doctor named Potter in our village. He was perhaps the sixth person I asked about summer employment, but to my relief he agreed to let me deliver medicines to his patients. This would save a good deal of his time, and he offered me five shillings a week. The wage was disappointing, but I had to take it.

Our village was named Landrum after the family that still owned much of the land. It was part of our parish. Dr Potter's practice extended to the neighbouring parish across the stream. People in the two parishes didn't mix much and any mixing usually involved fights. There was a legend about a war between the two parishes, but the legend was so confused, it was impossible to say if "parishes" were fighting or tribes.

Since I had to deliver medicines to both parishes, this would provoke hostilities, and I worried when I had to go across the stream. I hoped my task would allow me to travel unmolested, so carried the box of drugs in front of me as a sign of my good intentions.

There was hostility, mostly in the form of looks and occasional remarks, which I ignored. I began to realize that my family was considered outsiders despite centuries or probably millennia of residence in our own parish. This was strange, yet helpful in letting me do my job.

Otherwise, I was about every day in all weathers. The two parishes covered a considerable area, so my five shillings a week was hard earned. I had to spend some of my earnings to repair my shoes, so I would be taking even less to the grammar school.

Having little money worried me, as did the fact that I would be meeting and having to deal with an entirely unfamiliar group of boys and more difficult subjects to boot. Still I was excited also, for I hoped I was on my way to a better life.

SCHOOL DAYS

Despite the distance, I would have to walk all of it carrying my things. So I left early, just after breakfast, no farewell or last minute advice: my father was getting ready for start of term himself. I walked and walked, becoming very sweaty and tired.

I was assigned a "room" as I was in the lower fifth form, but the walls and door were so flimsy it was more of a courtesy room. Still, it was mine. I introduced myself to the other students, to universal disinterest. My "house" was in the charge of a monitor who was assisted or seconded by four proctors. All were in the upper sixth form. Since I was in the fifth form, I was not expected to fag for anyone, but on the other hand, I would not have the services of a fag. Since I didn't want to be bothered with having to deal with such a servant, I was content with this.

The two proctors I met seemed determined to make me feel unwelcome and unworthy. I had some experience at games, a plus, but was the son of a schoolmaster, a large minus. Then the monitor appeared and introduced himself as David Threlfall. He asked me about myself and told me briefly about himself, the school and its customs. He seemed moderately friendly and I warmed to him. It appeared I had been assigned to a good house and I was quite reassured. So I began the next stage of my education.

As I expected, the work was hard. Also the meals were poor and limited in quantity. Still, they weren't much worse than those prepared by the woman servant who "did for" us at my home. And I was prepared to work hard. David Threlfall was willing to answer my questions about courses, masters and the other students. This was helpful but I told myself to bother him as little as possible, as I didn't want to "wear out my welcome" as it were.

There were six houses in the school. These competed against each other in games. Since I tended toward awkwardness, my contributions to the matches were of variable value. Still I did my best, accepting bruises, sprains and occasionally being knocked down. My stoicism earned me a measure of respect, which made me feel I was part of the school.

The monitor of one of the other houses was a neighbour in a sense: Peter Landrum, the heir to the estate. He was actually Lord Peter Landrum, but it was an understood thing to call him "Landrum". He appeared to be taller than he was. This was because of his carriage, very erect, lofty even, very self-assured. In fact, he was just an inch or so taller than I. He had the typical fair English colouration, sharp, clean features, aristocratic features complete with sneer. However, it was his behaviour during games that compelled my attention.

He had a reputation for meanness and I did not like him. Though he would not do anything clearly considered unfair, I learned he needed to be watched and avoided if possible. I began to think he was singling me out for kicks, elbows, punches, etc. and guessed he knew who I was. Again, however, I had to endure, and did.

At meals, fags were expected to attend their masters, and I noticed Landrum's fag was a short, slight boy, probably in the second or third form but he looked even younger. What struck me particularly about this boy was his white-faced strained expression.

Also he moved stiffly. This provoked comments from some of the other students in my house.

By now I was aware that some of the boys were in sexual relationships with each other. I myself had been solicited once or twice to have such a relationship but had no interest at all; in fact I went so far as to obtain two wooden wedges to further secure the door to my room, for instances of forced sodomy were not unknown. I was certainly by then interested in sex, but with females. My imaginings of such seemed to occupy a great deal of my thoughts, and though I was ashamed of this, these dreams, fantasies and longings continued.

I knew that sometimes fags were compelled to submit to being sodomized or to participate in other forms of sexual gratification, so Landrum's fag was referred to as "Landrum's whore" or his "bugger boy". I wasn't sure whether these comments were derogatory or envious, but I felt sorry for the lad. He clearly wasn't happy with the situation and I once again was thankful I wasn't in Landrum's house.

Otherwise, my problems apart from the work were financial. I figured I could spend a shilling a week and last both terms, so tried to avoid eating anything not served at table. Since the other boys seemed to expect me to treat them occasionally, I had to be very careful about accepting pies, tarts and such from others. So I got a reputation for aloofness. I tried to explain my situation, but I wasn't sure my explanations were accepted.

So for one reason or another, I spent considerable time at my studies. Again, this did not enhance my popularity and I was unhappy about this. I tried to overcome these impressions by being friendly, by offering to help other boys with their lessons. This procured me a great deal of extra work but not much gratitude. All in all, my days in the grammar school were the reverse of "carefree" and I wondered how anyone could describe their time in a boarding school in such terms.

I returned to my home for the Holidays with some relief, not much, as I knew I must shortly return. Dr Potter very much wanted my services again,—though not so much that he was willing to pay me more for them—and I managed to collect a few more shillings delivering medicines to his patients. So I was about in the cold and the rain, but the alternative was staying at home with my father which would have been very depressing when it wasn't dull. He had in fact no comment at all by which I guessed my marks were satisfactory.

With the extra money, I tried to purchase a bit of popularity with my fellows. Still, my money seemed to melt away far too rapidly and I again retreated socially. It was, I guessed, very fortunate that meals at my home were so unappetizing. I was able to endure the meals served by the school better than most of my fellows.

There was one noteworthy change the second term: Landrum's fag did not return. This was commented upon at some length. Then, a rumour spread that the boy was dead, that he had died over the Holidays. At services we were bidden to include him in our prayers, so evidently the rumour was true. A few days later, another rumour: the boy had drowned. This was very surprising, as the weather hardly encouraged swimming. Then we heard that Landrum's fag had killed himself, had left a suicide note naming Landrum as the reason for his despair. The Coroner's Court said he was "of unsound mind", for reasons the Landrum family wanted unmentioned. The source of all this information was a lower sixth former whose father was an attorney, one who was close to the Coroner. The sixth former heard that money had changed hands, though I didn't like to think a Coroner's findings could be influenced in such a way.

Landrum himself seemed subdued—worried. Then he disappeared; again, rumours indicated he had been sent down. His monitor's status was insufficient to protect him, and, we speculated, the headmaster was not bribeable. I was glad to see the last of the fellow, but felt sorry for the boy and his parents. Aside from that, I really didn't want to think about what the boy had endured.

My second term otherwise was similar to my first. I was better able to deal with the work. And the games, though still played hard, were not played meanly. In fact, an element of sportsmanship crept in, most welcome to me and I think to all of us. Financially and socially the end of term left me with sixpence and still no real friends.

I returned with shoes badly needing repair yet had to take up my deliveries for Dr Potter once more. It had rained a great deal and the creek that separated the two parishes constituting Potter's practice was high, hindering my deliveries. I spent the first three weeks with wet feet by day, trying to dry my shoes and stockings by night. My father was as uncommunicative as usual, and I wondered how he had been able to persuade my mother to marry him.

I was struck, for the first time, by the fact that the inhabitants of the two parishes spoke with distinct dialects, and also used distinctive expressions. It seemed very strange, since these people had been living next each other for centuries if not millennia yet kept apart from each other. There were distinct differences in customs as well.

In fact, I sometimes heard people of that parish humming or whistling various airs, airs quite different from the ones sung or whistled in our parish. The inhabitants of the two parishes might as well have been from different countries and permanently hostile countries at that.

There was a pretty girl in one of the cottages I was delivering to in the next parish, and I tried to become acquainted with her. She was not encouraging: I lived in the wrong parish and was a Mendy to boot. This was very frustrating: being rejected for such reasons hurt me greatly, and I spent the summer in useless daydreams. I very much wanted a sweetheart, and this girl had captured my fancy. I began to think about how I might become a more attractive suitor, not in terms of appearance, but in terms of income, of prestige. And more, at this moment I understood I wanted to be accepted, admired, not merely tolerated. And for me this also meant education.

Becoming a schoolmaster like my father, if I wanted a better position, that is in a public school or university, meant reading at university. And that meant money. Money I didn't have. And what subject was I to read? On my deliveries, I began to wonder about becoming a doctor like Potter. He was just about the only other man in the two parishes with an education, and if I was going to have to work so hard in school, I might as well work to some purpose.

If Potter had a daughter about my age, I would have paid court to her. However his children were grown and gone, leaving him and his wife. I began to pay more attention to what he said to his patients, what they told him and tried to connect these to the medicines I was delivering. If he was at leisure, I would ask questions about symptoms and treatments. He seemed to like to talk, and I guessed his wife had no interest in the practice of medicine.

I asked him how one became a doctor, and he told me. As I feared, it sounded expensive: five years at university to qualify. There were evidently no scholarships for the study of medicine, and it sounded impossible for me. So I returned to the upper fifth form very discouraged.

David Threlfall had graduated, as had the proctors who had made me feel unwelcome, a mixed result. The new monitor and proctors basically ignored me, which was as well. I met my acquaintances—I didn't think of them as friends—and we discussed the summer's events. I hadn't much to say as all I had done was work. Some of the other boys had spent their time at games or traveling, one or two to the Continent. I wished once again my family had money or connections. One or two of the boys asked me if I had seen Landrum over the summer. I had not and no wish to. Evidently he had gone up to Oxford despite not graduating our school; I imagined his family could get him admitted there. I decided I would go to the University of London and qualify as a doctor rather than go to Oxford and read anything.

To this end, it would have been helpful if my school offered courses in the sciences, but as a grammar school the basic offerings were Latin and Greek. I did my best, I had to keep my marks up, but preparation for medicine was entirely lacking. I would have to try to pay much more attention to how Dr Potter carried out his practice. I wondered if he could recommend me or sponsor me.

My second year passed, hour by hour, day by day. Home for the Holidays, I worked again for Potter during deliveries, but when there was an opportunity, I would ask him about his patients, their symptoms and what the symptoms meant. I hoped he was beginning to see me as a sort of apprentice, which in generations past would have been enough to qualify me.

On one journey to a patient in the adjoining parish, I had to cross the stream of course. It was high and I heard a faint crying. Looking about, I saw a tiny kitten stranded on a rock. It was soaked, bedraggled and frightened. I rescued the creature with considerable difficulty and at some risk to myself. We had no pets at home; presumably my father didn't want the expense. The animal clawed its way inside my coat and nested there. I guessed someone was drowning a litter and this one survived. My delivery was to an elderly lady. I was admitted, presented the medicine, and the kitten emerged, crying. The woman stared at the kitten, then held out her hands and plucked it from my coat. She seemed quite taken with it, telling me it was the image of her cat that had died a few months ago. She caressed the creature, which began to purr. I assured the woman the kitten was gratis, which she smiled at, and it occurred to me that the kitten was in a sense much better medicine for a lonely old woman than could be obtained from any apothecary. On returning, I mentioned this to Potter. I hoped he was favourably impressed with my insight.

Back at school, I was increasingly frustrated by the curriculum but was trapped. Once more, I had to endure. I was becoming better at games by dint of practice. And the physical activity was helpful, leaving me less restless, less plagued by thoughts of girls. Otherwise I worked very hard, becoming known as a "swot".

Returning to my job with Dr Potter after term ended, I found him busier with the casualties from a brawl between some of the young men of the two parishes. This was a fairly frequent occurrence: about 1 May, both parishes undertook Morris dancing, harmless enough in itself, but after considerable drinking, some of the men from my parish attempted a sort of raid on the adjoining one. The idea was to cross the stream and seize something, a branch from a tree, a stone would be enough, and of course the men from the adjoining parish would try to stop our men. The priests from the two parishes tried to prevent this, calling it pagan, with indifferent success.

Aside from deliveries, I began to accompany Potter to both parishes. This was to help with bandaging, fashioning splints, etc. for some of the injuries were serious. There were no deaths this time, but there had been occasional fatalities, all commemorated in tavern talk, helping keep rancour alive. Walking to the adjoining parish, I was constantly reminded of the hostility of many there, even though I was a Mendy. I felt much safer when I was with Potter.

With feelings stirred up by the latest brawl, I feared my deliveries alone to the neighbour parish would be even less welcome. So it proved. I had to stop near a pub to retie one of my shoes. This required me to set my protective box of medicines down.

A fellow about my own age said, "Yer not welcome here. Get quit."

I was annoyed but tried to be polite, saying, "Some sick people in this parish need these medicines and I must deliver them."

He had moved close to me, clearly not appeased, and then suddenly swung his fist at me. I ducked enough so his fist hit me a glancing blow on the side of my head. In turn I drove forward at him, hitting his breastbone with my elbow. This knocked him back and he fell. He lay, winded, cursing weakly. Some other men had gathered, watching. Since my attacker was harmless for the moment, I extended my hand to help him get up. This was customary at my school but surprised him. However, once up, he called me "Mendy bisturd" and moved off. The other men watching were hostile but did nothing. I could pick up my box and continue, making sure I wasn't being followed.

I didn't feel any satisfaction in winning a fight. I knew the situation was unstable, that I could be set upon by several. However I realized that all the time I had spent at games, especially having to deal with Landrum's tactics, had saved me from a beating. Even so, I returned by a different route.

Otherwise, I did feel I was learning something of medicine. I was paid the same, but feared complaining. This despite being of much more use, as I imagined Potter might begin charging me for his instruction. So I returned to the school for the lower sixth form in exactly the same financial condition as for the fifth forms.

I was now eligible to have a fag myself. However, employment of fags also required money, for fags were often sent to buy things for their masters, usually things to eat, and it was the custom to tip the fag. So I gave the fellow assigned to me my "name and liberties" as the saying was, meaning if any other upper form student asked him to perform some errand, the fellow could say he was doing something for me. In addition, I advised the fellow to concentrate on his studies. I had no idea how scrupulously my advice would be followed, but that was no concern of mine.

My first term in the lower sixth was identical, save for accidental differences, all minor. I began to hope my marks and conduct might lead to my being house monitor. I wasn't sure why I wanted this. However it was an honour and I coveted honours, even though I couldn't think why.

Returning home at the Holidays, I found a major change: the servant who had "done for us" as long as I remembered had died. Her place was taken by a much younger woman, trim figure but rather hard-featured. Her name was Ellen. Since she was relatively young and not actually repulsive, I became interested in her. However, Ellen was not interested in me and I was too shy and awkward to court her anyway. So I pursued my job with Dr Potter and returned at the end of the Holidays feeling I had learned a little more about medicine and its practice.

Second term proceeded much as the two preceding second terms had. I had hoped to be named at least a proctor to my house but other students were named. The headmaster wasn't in the habit

17

of giving his reasons for these appointments and I shrank from asking him. I concluded I simply wasn't sufficiently "popular" or perhaps authoritative, so would not be accepted by the other boys as a leader. I was very cast down by this, surprisingly so. However, I said nothing as was my custom.

The summer, my last as a grammar school student, was wet, rainy and unpleasant. My shoes needed more repairs, further limiting the money I would take back to the school. Otherwise I noticed my father and the servant, Ellen, were talking to each other, most unusual in the case of my father. My presence appeared to inhibit these conversations, but the weather restricted my walks, even if I had the energy. I began to sense my presence was unwelcome, which seemed odd. However, once the summer was over, I would be away at school. Ellen, like our previous servant, kept up our garden, growing vegetables. Since our household had little money, I had come to associate vegetables with poverty, but perforce had to eat them or starve. I noticed one change Ellen had made, however: she had also planted some flowers, in particular a rose bush near a shed where garden utensils were kept. My father did not object to this, so I had to accept it.

During my last summer, I had written to University College, London, to inquire about fees and expenses to pursue a medical education. The reply had further discouraged me; also I would have to take and pass an exam to matriculate. More expense, and where could I get the money? I decided I would have to talk to my father, much as I disliked the prospect. I would also speak to Dr Potter and risk the likely rebuff.

Fall was dry, good weather for games. Except for these, I buried myself in work. I really couldn't afford much else. Once or twice I actually had conversations with some fellow sixth formers, conversations about our futures. Most of them were going into the Indian Civil Service, a few to Oxford or Cambridge. I was the only one interested in pursuing a profession and I confessed my fears of being quite unable to afford this. My fellows seemed sympathetic, which surprised me. However, since I had never confided in them about this before, perhaps I was naïve. Still, I returned home for the Holidays in a better frame of mind.

This did not last long. First, I observed that Ellen was "with child", several months along, obviously by my father. I had no idea about my father's legal status; was he still married to my mother or not? And if he was legally married, how much would a divorce cost? Even so, I had to ask him if he could provide some money for my further education. I explained my ambition, told him how much tuition and expenses were, and asked for his help. This while Ellen sat in the chair my mother had sat in, sewing as my mother had done.

My father seemed embarrassed about the situation, pointed out that he would have to support Ellen and my half-brother or -sister, but finally said he thought he could provide £300. Evidently he had been able to save something over the years. He kept looking toward Ellen as he told me this, but Ellen nodded. Permission had been granted, evidently. I was very grateful to both of them, and told them so. £300 would help a great deal. I guessed that, after 14 years absence, my mother could be considered as having abandoned my father, but the legalities of his state were unclear to me and possibly to him and Ellen.

My talk with Potter was less satisfactory. His practice supported him and his wife so was worth money. I couldn't guess how much, but I couldn't ask him to borrow on that. He seemed averse to loaning me money, so I went away on my deliveries with only the promise from my father.

Walking past the high meadow my ancestors had lived on, I saw a hunt was going on. The Landrums were out with their guests in pursuit of game. The good man's croft seemed to crouch on the horizon while horses streamed by. I wondered if deer or any game ventured into it. However, this time I did see birds in the trees. I saw crows, jackdaws and ravens, quite noisy. I even saw two or three red kites. I guessed there was carrion in the good man's croft, so some land animals must go into the place.

My last term was spent concentrating on my marks, hoping for some prizes. Games were for release, for escape from schoolwork.

A few conversations with some colleagues were otherwise all I had, but were comforting to me and I hope to the others as well.

Ultimately, I won only one prize, in Greek. I was presented with a copy of Aristophanes' plays. I was very disappointed but of course had to congratulate the winners of the other prizes. My father wasn't there; I felt quite alone. I returned to the house very dejected.

My "stepmother", if that was her status, had delivered a girl, my half-sister. She was named Rose, I didn't know why, just that the name meant something to my "stepmother" and my father. Looking at them, I saw their expressions soften when they looked at each other, a sign of real affection. This was nice yet it left me feeling I wasn't as much a part of the household as before. My father told me I was expected to help, foster and protect my half-sister. I nodded. What else could I do? Given the difference in our ages, the girl would effectively have two fathers.

I returned to my job, delivering medicines and helping Potter any way I could. I would have to travel to London to take the Matriculation Exam to enrol in University College. While I was fairly confident I would be admitted, still it was a source of worry, also expense.

One morning I was carrying my box of medicines, walking along the lane that led past the fields encompassing the high meadow and good man's croft. Sheep were grazing in the fields. Ahead three men on horseback were approaching. I recognized one: Landrum. He was atop a great bay. He saw me, urged his horse ahead, pulled it to a stop, just inches from me, and sat sneering at me. His two companions also pulled up.

One of the two companions said, "Here, steady on, Landrum," as Landrum's horse had nearly knocked me down.

"And what are you doing here, Mendy?" Landrum asked.

I said, "Delivering medicines to sick people."

This took Landrum by surprise. Then he urged his horse forward, showering me with bits of dirt. For an instant, I thought he was going to hit me with his riding crop. His two companions looked somewhat apologetic, and followed him.

I shook myself and continued on my way. Occasional bits of dirt fell off me, dislodged by my movement. I was somewhat shaken by the encounter but became angrier as I proceeded. I hadn't heard anything about Landrum my last three years at school. I didn't know whether he had taken a degree or what he was reading. However, I stayed out of pubs, so wouldn't have heard the gossip. As the heir, his doings would be discussed at length. I guessed he regarded me as an enemy, though I could not imagine why.

Taking the Matriculation Exam cost me two weeks wages in effect. However, ten shillings was a trifle compared with what I would need, assuming I was admitted. And I knew little about the Exam, so didn't know what to study. Consequently, on the train to London, my anxiousness increased by the mile, and trips to the loo on the train did not help.

In the room the Exam was given, I had to read and reread the first question or two before attempting to answer. Since the Exam was timed, this heightened my fears. However, I noticed some of the questions on the Latin and Greek parts were similar to questions I had to answer at school (one was identical), so provided I could remember what I had written . . . But once I had gotten into the Exam, things went better and better as I came up to speed, mentally.

We were tested on our knowledge of Latin, Greek, English and mathematics. Coming as I did from a grammar school, I eventually had no problems with the Latin and Greek, and I had noticed my studies of Latin had been very helpful with English grammar and vocabulary. So that meant no problems there either. I had worked hard at mathematics as well: I had the notion that knowledge of mathematics made me somehow more capable, more in control, and I was able to answer all the maths questions also. As a result, I left the room the Matriculation Exam had been given in feeling emptied, intellectually speaking, otherwise shaken and exhausted. After my return, the summer proceeded as the four past summers had.

A letter arrived from the Registrar. I held it, trying to gauge from its weight and thickness whether I had been admitted. Finally I forced myself to open and read it. At first the writing, the letters, made no sense. Then I forced calmness on myself and discovered I had been admitted. This was a relief, but only for a short time: I still had to figure how to make £300 and odd last five years in London. Still, I could continue my journey.

On inquiry, I had found some scholarships were available, though only for the first two years. I would need a letter of recommendation from the headmaster of my school, so had to lose another shilling, trekking to the school and back. The headmaster seemed sympathetic, and promised me a strong recommendation. This surprised me, but was gratifying. He was kind enough to say I had missed out on three other prizes each by only a few marks—also gratifying. Potter said he would recommend me as well, which could only help. Consequently the last few weeks of the summer were anxious but hopeful.

Another letter arrived from the University. Again I hesitated to open it, afraid of a crushing disappointment. Again I told myself to be a man, getting rejected for a scholarship could hardly be the worst trial I would face. Finally I tore the envelope open, extracted the letter inside, opened it and forced myself to read it. It was good news: my first year's tuition was remitted, and if my marks were satisfactory, the second year's tuition would be remitted also. This meant I had perhaps three years of the five covered.

I showed the letter to my father and he nodded. The £300 would be needed after all. Still I had a hint he was pleased: I might not graduate but would at least have some university behind me. At worst I could get a job teaching in a public school, a more prestigious and somewhat better paying job than his. Ellen smiled at the two of us and my father actually embraced her. Not exactly a celebration, but at least good cheer.

So I wrote letters to the headmaster and to Potter, thanking them. I also said I would do my utter best to merit their and my father's support, and I meant that.

UNIVERSITY

---◆---

My visit to London to take the Matriculation Exam had been short. I had the impression of smells: smoke from chimneys and motors, along with horse dung. Everything and everybody were moving quickly. Living in the capitol confirmed this: London was sooty and smoky and fast. Also noisy: sometimes humming, sometimes roaring, ebbing and cresting unpredictably, a cacophonous tangle of sounds. I had to become accustomed to this, however. If buildings had been up for a while, perhaps as little as a few months, stone and masonry alike assumed a grey-brown shade like the colour of the air much of the time. New buildings were brightly coloured—for a while—vivid red brick, often.

I had read about London, its intense fogs for example, in Dickens' works among others. But living there, after coming from countryside, was another thing. I developed a permanent cough or constant throat-clearing that I had to control in lecture halls, vexing and distracting. Still, just another thing I had to endure.

For my return to London, I took £50. I would need food, lodging and books. I hoped to keep my spending under that, telling myself that my father had worked years to put that money by and I wanted to respect his sacrifice. The cheapest room I could rent cost six shillings a week, coal was extra. I did without coal, instead sleeping under a mound of every piece of clothing I possessed. I went without breakfast, often without lunch, trying to keep spending for dinner below a shilling. So my diet was starchy and flavourless and poor. My lodgings were only fractionally above squalid.

My main problem was with my courses. These were entirely science courses, utterly foreign to me in content and vocabulary. Consequently I struggled. I tried to compensate by writing everything down, memorizing everything I heard in the lectures or read in the textbooks. Some things, some ideas made little sense. Though the reasoning was foreign to me, by dint of repetition and working all the waking hours, the material gradually became at least more familiar.

The labs (chemistry, physics and biology) were a trial as well. My dexterity was quite limited, most frustrating. I had to force patience on myself, repeat procedures whenever I could. Yet the major problem the labs posed for me was the time they consumed. With the demands on my understanding of the material as well, there really seemed too few hours in a day.

Once again I was isolating myself from my fellow students. This was itself depressing, particularly since some of the "fellows" were women. Dealing with them in any way was awkward for me, another isolating influence.

With the help of old exams, I began to see what I was supposed to be able to do; in fact the material began to make much more sense. Things started falling into place and I finished the term with some credit. So I returned to a more comfortable house, much better meals and the prospect of earning a few more shillings. This cheered me, though Ellen was concerned at my loss of weight and pasty complexion. I agreed I would spend somewhat more on food.

I had been told and believed that at least £500, perhaps as much as £1000 would be needed. The medical schools in the provinces, such as those at Leeds and Manchester, were somewhat cheaper but not much. I wanted a London degree if I could get one.

The major expense was tuition and fees. Not much I could do about those. Food and lodging offered very limited scope for economy, but such measures had to be taken. On the train going back to London it occurred to me that buying tinned stuff would be cheaper (and probably more nourishing) than meals at restaurants. So when I arrived in London, I bought a tin opener and a spoon at an ironmonger, and then went to a grocer and purchased a few tins, mostly vegetables as these were cheapest.

My idea was successful as far as keeping expenses for food down, though I had to eat everything cold. Still, for less than a shilling a day, I could have at least two meals a day, necessary as I found that going without breakfast and lunch left me weak and shaky by dinner. I could even have an occasional tin of beef stew and tinned fruit two or three times a week. Of course, once the tin was opened, I had to eat it all. Even so, with one term's experience behind me, I was able to improve my diet without spending more. And the course work was now much easier, both because of what I had learned first term and because my studying was more efficient. Still, the exams at the end of my second term were harder, longer, designed to weed out the weaker students, and I returned home exhausted.

Once more on my rounds, I didn't see Landrum again. No loss there. Otherwise, I was now more accepted, both sides of the boundary stream, so could pursue my task with less fear of obstruction. Being a Mendy did have some advantages,—no, more like fewer liabilities. My pay from Potter was unchanged, but I was beginning to feel much more confident. I could at least get a B. A. with what my father had promised me, but I wanted a M. B. to qualify as a doctor. Aside from my own inclinations, that is how I promised him I would use his money.

Ellen, my presumed step-mother, made me two shirts and repaired my other clothes so I would look more as though I slept under a roof, rather than on the Embankment. This was very thoughtful and kind of her. I guessed her efforts were less for me than for my father; all the same, I greatly appreciated her work. On the other hand, my shoes were by now beyond repair so I had to buy new. Since my scholarship was renewed, and since I had managed to complete my first year spending less than £40 of the £50 I had taken with me, I was confident of finishing the first two years. So I took only £50 with me for my second year. For the three years of "doing the rounds" I would have almost £200, not enough, but I was feeling something would "turn up".

In this Micawber-ish mood, I began my second year, or third term. Once again, the early weeks were spent feeling overwhelmed. As the term proceeded, I began to get on top of the material and even felt I had time to attend a play, one of Oscar Wilde's. I had been given the ticket. I enjoyed it very much. I was better dressed, so did not feel particularly conspicuous. Still, I left feeling unhappy as there were many attractive young women there and I wished very much one of them was my sweetheart. For that, however, money was lacking, as always seemed to be the case.

My last term on scholarship was easier and I now had time to attend two more plays—gratis seats—and to hold a few conversations with fellow students. I was surprised to find several of them were as pinched financially as I. We exchanged ideas and information on cheap meals and lodging, some which might be helpful.

The summer was spent as in years past, extracting five shillings a week from Dr Potter. When there was time, I would question him about symptoms and procedures, drugs and prognoses. Though garrulous, he was only moderately informative. However, since he was my only source of how medicine was actually practiced—and I was beginning to understand what was meant by that expression—I listened very attentively.

The University sent me a letter midsummer informing me my marks were sufficient to allow me to continue towards obtaining a M. B. In fact, once I completed the three years of "rounds" I would take a second, second-class honours. This was moderately good news: a first would have been much better, but considering how poorly prepared I had been, was actually reasonably good. Even better, I was considered to have passed my first qualifying exam. This left the second qualifying exam to be taken probably at the end of the third year of study, with the final qualifying exam at the end of the fifth year. My father and step-mother were pleased. Saving always the question of paying for the three years, my way was clear.

I took another instalment, £100, with me on my return to London. With what I had managed to avoid spending the first two years, plus my meagre earnings from Potter, I had nearly £130. Aside from paying the tuition and fees, about £100, I had to buy professional equipment such as a stethoscope. For dissections, I had to have scalpels, etc. There were also other fees, and considering I had to eat and sleep some place, I constantly worried that the money I had wouldn't be enough.

With remission of the tuition, I had managed to complete the first two years, spending less than £60. With what I earned working for Potter, I had a little less than £250 left. This would certainly be enough for one year and perhaps half of a second, but I would need at least £200 more, or so I imagined. I returned for my third year, feeling anxious.

MAUD

In addition I soon found I would need a costume, so I looked like a doctor. I had to buy a black coat and trousers and suitable cravat. This was the custom. Talking to some fellow students, I learned that the cheapest course was to buy second-hand. As soon as I had time, I went to a place that sold used clothing, a place that carried what I needed. Generations of medical students had patronized this shop.

There was a young woman behind the counter. She was short, slight, "elfin" actually, dark haired, with large dark eyes. She was also a very pretty girl, perhaps twenty or so. I told her what I needed.

She nodded and asked, "What size?" This confused me, and I finally admitted I didn't know. So she called for her father, "Pa!" He came out from where he had been working, pulled a tape measure from around his neck and measured me. He spoke some numbers to the girl, who removed a coat, waistcoat and trousers from a hanger. I was able to try on the coat. It looked all right, fit me, the trousers seemed long enough, and the ensemble was fairly cheap, 7/6. I paid. The girl, I learned, was named Maud, Maud Millen. However, there was nothing more I could do in aid of expanding our acquaintance, at least nothing I could think of, so I left with my purchases.

I had to find a place to live, well, a place to sleep. Meals other than from tins I could take at the hospital. These were quite cheap, though monotonous. I had never liked stewed rabbit, but that was what was usually served. I had also learned that a few students actually slept in hospital, in unused beds or under stairwells. This practice was tolerated by the governors. We could bathe in the surgeons' shower baths, so had to pay only for laundry, and there were laundresses in the hospital that would do this for a fee. So my living costs would be quite low, a great relief to me.

At least the fees were fixed. I learned that students once had to directly pay the physicians the students followed on rounds, and in guineas, not pounds. Everything else was quite expensive: the costs of the cadavers we dissected, the equipment we had to buy, all evidently priced assuming we were rich or would be. Still, I had the money—for my first year of clinical work, my third year in London.

I was in the University College Medical School. The building was new. It had several lecture rooms but also many students. Our anatomy instructors, like all the students, were men. The result was lectures that were extraordinarily vulgar. Filthy mnemonic verses were routinely presented to help us remember names of anatomical features. This was amusing but would lead to a certain separation between us and any female relations, actual or potential.

For our course in anatomy, we had to buy a cadaver. These were expensive, about £15. Since cadavers were usually shared, I went in with two other students to buy one. This was a man, a relatively old man, as were most of the cadavers. I secretly hoped for a woman, perhaps a suicide, a young woman, for I wanted to gaze at a naked woman. I was ashamed of this desire but listening to my colleagues, I discovered my fantasies and longings were quite mundane compared with those of some of my fellow students.

In the event, though a few female cadavers were obtained, these were, like nearly all the male ones, of old people, worn and withered. These were still of some prurient interest, though this rapidly dissipated once we started to work. The room we did the dissections in was large, lit by electric lamps. There were skylights but no windows. In the room were numerous tables, each with three or four chairs about them, most with a body lying atop. On the walls were a great many drawings of progressive stages of dissections: of the throat, the chest, the abdomen, etc. Everyone smoked cigars or pipes. Everyone save me that is: tobacco cost money. The smoking was a defence against the overpowering smell of the preservative employed, and a much more offensive smell of putrefaction. The idea, commented on at some length, that we were all destined to rot, to putrefy, to become offensive, was made the subject for what is called "gallows humour". Otherwise, we worked very long and hard at the dissection table, gradually reducing our cadaver to fragments.

Talking to some of my colleagues, I was surprised to find many of them to be older than I was. In fact, a few of these had left school for a year or more to earn money to continue their education. So I was not alone in my plight. We often discussed methods for saving money or earning more between terms, nothing revelatory but in a way comforting. Most of my older colleagues, however, had failed a qualifying exam, some more than once. I was very surprised to learn that, as a "Grecian", my academic qualifications were considered superior to those of most of my colleagues.

We lived in an atmosphere of tobacco smoke and preservative in the dissecting rooms, an atmosphere that accompanied us everywhere, so that our course of study was obvious to anyone within a few feet of us. If we wanted to attend a play or a concert, or even accompany some doctors on their rounds, we required a change of clothes as well as frequent shower baths. Still, there was nothing for it but to pay whatever was demanded.

I went again to the Millen's clothing store for a second suit to be worn outside the dissection room, about the same price as before. Miss Millen's father wasn't about, so I was able to talk to Miss Millen about non-commercial subjects such as whether she ever attended plays or concerts. She was cautiously forthcoming about her interests. She had attended a few public lectures and free concerts on Sundays with some other girls. I gathered she was intelligent, alert to what was happening in Britain and not adamantly averse to attending some things with me. I had a little more time this year to do such things; the question was of course money. I decided to see what was on offer and ask her if she would attend whatever it was with me.

Events Sunday afternoons were all I could ask her to, so I could escort her back while it was still light. Throw in the requirement that they are free and close, and the selection became quite limited. Hunting through yesterday's newspapers, I found a free concert for Sunday week that was close enough. I went to her father's shop as soon as I had time and told her of the concert, the selections offered, and requested the honour of her company. Her father was attending another customer, but must have heard us. Miss Millen looked at him to see if he objected. Evidently he didn't so she agreed to go with me. We settled on a time I would call, she told me where she lived and I left feeling both relieved and anxious.

I wasn't sure of the customs of these excursions and asked some of my colleagues. There wasn't much anyone had to say. I would bring an umbrella and might have to take her to eat somewhere, probably a chips shop. Beyond that I was on my own. One colleague gave me some advice I thought sound: don't try to be entertaining or clever or to try to impress her. As a potential doctor, I should be able to support a wife in reasonable style and this, I was told, was sufficient for most women. I thought that a cynical point of view but hoped it was correct.

Our conversation returned to the usual topics, not women but diseases, causes, symptoms, treatments, the quirks of the men we followed on rounds, ways of earning money; as I said, the usual topics. I was finding those conversations entertaining and useful, professionally speaking. I tried very hard to note and remember everything we saw or were told, and sometimes I was able to contribute positively to our conversations, giving value for money as it were.

The Sunday I was to call on Miss Millen was clear and bright, not too cold, so I left the umbrella. Otherwise I took unwonted care with my appearance, having a shower bath, shaving, wearing my best professional garb. I was too nervous to eat much. I called on her at the agreed time, meeting her mother. That lady looked me over keenly but said little. Miss Millen and I set out to walk to the concert as it wasn't far.

I was silent as I didn't think anything I had to say could be considered even interesting still less entertaining. The silence was broken by Miss Millen, "I don't remember what you said your name was."

I was confused, almost giving my name as Millen, but finally got out, "Mendy, David Mendy."

"Where are you from, Mr Mendy?"

I replied, "Gloucestershire. Near Cirencester. The upper Thames valley."

More silence until she said, "How much longer will you be studying medicine?"

I was tempted to say it was a lifelong study but remembered my instructions, so said, "This year is my third; I have two more after this one."

"And then you will be a doctor?"

I said, "Yes. At that point I can legally treat patients and charge for the treatment. So hopefully I will be able to make a living."

We crossed a street. She asked me, "Where will you practice?"

I shook my head, said, "Wherever I can. Perhaps where I grew up, I know the area and the people. But right now I am focussed on my studies and on paying for them." I didn't know why I said that, except it occupied a great deal of my thoughts.

She caught what I said and asked, "What does your father do?"

I replied, "He teaches at a Council school. He said he could contribute £300 toward my education so I will have to find the rest."

"How much will that be?"

I thought, wondering how we had gotten into this conversation, and eventually said, "I am fairly sure of having enough for my fourth year. After that, say £130 should be enough. After my fourth year, I can work as a doctor, under the supervision of a qualified physician. Miss Millen, I apologize for bringing up such a matter. I wasn't thinking of what I should, which is you and your entertainment."

She glanced at me, commented, "As a shopkeeper's daughter, I am well aware of the importance of money, of making a living." A few steps, then she asked, "Do you have brothers or sisters? Does your mother work?"

This was awkward, but I couldn't think of any way of avoiding a reply, so said, "My mother deserted us when I was four. My father recently remarried." I decided to give him and Ellen the benefit of the doubt. "And I now have a half-sister. My stepmother keeps the house. Have you any brothers or sisters?"

Miss Millen replied, "I have an older brother who is a sailor. He is now a second mate on a merchant ship."

"Is he married?" I asked.

"No. I don't know if he is seeing anyone. We don't hear much from him, as he is at sea most of the time."

We arrived where the concert was to be given, found seats and sat down. I remembered I needed to procure programs, told Miss Millen this and got two. We looked at these in silence, broken by her comment, "I haven't heard anything by some of these composers."

I said, "Nor have I. Growing up, I never listened to music, so the few concerts I have heard so far have been a revelation."

This concert was no exception, some absolutely beautiful pieces or parts of pieces, very moving, smile inducing. There was an additional piece, an "encore", a military piece that had many in the audience clapping in unison. After, we herded out with everyone else. I was in a much brighter mood. What was it about music that did that?

I accompanied Miss Millen back to her residence. We walked in silence until she said, "I don't know if you have a dinner engagement. If not, I was told I could invite you to dine with us."

I was taken aback. Eventually, I came out with, "My dinner engagements consist of very cheap meals at the hospital accompanied by prolonged, sometimes uproarious conversations with colleagues." Finally I was able to say, "In other words, no, and I accept your kind invitation and thank you, and your parents."

I opened the door for Miss Millen and then followed her inside. She said, "Ma! Pa! Mr Mendy accepted our invitation." Mrs Millen was very like her daughter, short, very slight and dark. Her parents were welcoming and we sat down almost immediately to eat. I was reasonably confident of my table manners, so could savour the meal. It was several cuts above what I was accustomed to eat, and I told the Millens so. Mrs Millen seemed pleased.

The meal was dispatched fairly quickly, and then we adjourned to the parlour. Mrs Millen asked about the concert. I was rather fulsome in my description but remembered to attribute my happiness with the selection to my companion, which was well received. I learned that Miss Millen actually kept the books, Mr Millen cheerfully acknowledging he had no head for figures. This struck me as a very serious limitation in a businessman; evidently the daughter had been bookkeeper for some years, replacing Mrs Millen. Also Mrs Millen said Miss Millen had improved profits. I looked at Miss Millen with increased respect.

The Millens asked about my family and prospects and I told them what I had told their daughter, saving the part about currently lacking the money for the last year. They seemed pleased and I began to see I was being considered as a possible son-in-law. The daughter exhibited no particular emotion in this respect, so I really didn't know what to think. However, the parents were interested in my prospects for employment and I answered honestly, including where I simply didn't know. It now being dark and everyone needing to be at work tomorrow morning, I rose and sincerely thanked my hosts and companion before taking my leave.

Walking back to the hospital, I felt relieved. I guessed I had passed some sort of social acceptance exam and began wondering what I could take Miss Millen to in future. At least she seemed willing to accompany me. She was certainly a pretty girl, my guess as to her intelligence had been confirmed, but only time and experience would show if we really got on well. I had never had a "best girl" before and desired the experience very much.

So another element was added to my life. Aside from courses, dissections, doing rounds and discussing medicine, I pored over newspapers (yesterday's) for finding out to what I could take Miss Millen. She agreed to accompany me to another free Sunday concert.

This was indoors, which was just as well, as it rained. Once again I was invited to dinner at the Millens and once again I accepted. Besides that, however, I learned she was interested in social or political matters and also liked plays. So I added lectures on any topics that we could attend without paying. Plays always had to be paid for so were sampled rarely, unless someone gave me the tickets.

After the lectures, we would walk back to her parents' dwelling, talking about what we had heard. She was strongly in favour of women's suffrage, not surprisingly. We eventually agreed that extension of the franchise had to be done, but that violent tactics in furtherance of that cause were harmful to it and, indeed, wrong. In particular, breaking shop windows struck her, a shopkeeper's daughter, as totally uncalled for. I listened to her and discussed many such matters with her, my respect for her intelligence growing at each outing. I couldn't tell what she thought of me. I mentioned several times how frustrated my fear of paying relatively small amounts of money made me, but she seemed to support my struggle to make my father's money go as far as possible.

However, she was also well-read, and interested in literature. One of the free lectures we attended together was on "Female Characters in Victorian Literature." Unusually, this was given by a woman. After the lecture, Miss Millen and I walked back to her parents' house talking about what we had heard. The lecture had mentioned Lizzie Hexam, the heroine of Dickens's *Our Mutual Friend,* and this prompted me to criticize Dickens's handling of some of his characters:

"Perhaps because I have always had to strive, to work very hard, I sympathized with the schoolmaster who was in love with the heroine. I thought she should have been more sympathetic with his efforts. Instead, she was enthralled with Wrayburn, whose behaviour toward the schoolmaster was, in my opinion, cruel and unworthy of the name of 'gentleman.'"

Miss Millen replied:

"Women may sympathize with a man, but they want a man they can look up to, look up to in every way, a man who can take them away from the day-to-day, the ordinary. The same could be said about Amy Dorrit's love for Arthur Clennam instead of the boy she grew up with. I think that is the real essence of romance: a transformation or repudiation of reality."

We fell silent. I was wondering how to take what she said; was she telling me I was too ordinary, my life and prospects too like her own? By this time, we were at her parents' house, a decent meal beckoned, and after the meal we talked of other things.

Walking back to the hospital, I reflected that men were trapped by their circumstances, too. We often had to focus, perhaps too narrowly, on the day-to-day, but most men wanted at least a taste of adventure, experiences transcending our workaday lives, to "do high deeds in Hungary, to pass all men's believing." And were about as likely to achieve their dreams as women were, I thought as I headed to the place where I slept.

The term came to an end. I would return to my home once more, work for Potter for five shillings a week, work much more knowledgably now but for the same pay. I was beginning to understand that, as a physician, Potter had definite limitations. Some of his treatments were out of date. I wasn't sure how I could deal with such situations. Should I simply do as I was told, even though it was contrary to the best interests of the patient?

One of the men in my compartment was evidently a cleric. He was friendly, asked me where I was from and made some comments about the history of the area that indicated he was an antiquarian. I asked him, "Have you ever heard of the 'good man's croft'? There is a patch of forest nearby that has that name."

The cleric looked interested, said, "Yes, that was once a widespread custom, leaving some part of the land to the service of an evil spirit or spirits. I didn't realize any had survived, certainly not this far south. Where is this located?"

I answered, "It is part of the Landrum estate. A thoroughly spooky place."

The cleric smiled and said, "Having some archaeologists examine it might be very interesting. I will ask if the family is willing to have this done."

I said, "My great-great-grandfather said something to me just before he died that suggested child sacrifice was done." The cleric, now very interested, nodded. I went on, "I imagine the custom of the 'good man's croft' predates Christianity."

The cleric nodded again, said, "The Church opposed this custom, of course, and it had eventually disappeared as a result, or at least I thought it had."

We had stopped. Two people in our compartment left. Now it was just the cleric and I. I asked him, "Was that a Celtic custom?"

He shook his head, and then said, "No, such a custom was never associated with the Celts. I believe it occurred only in Britain, so it must be pre-Celtic. It could go back to the introduction of farming. The custom might have originated at the beginning of farming, in an effort to overcome the difficulties and uncertainties of a new practice—farming, I mean—by placating spirits of the land made unhappy by use of the land to grow crops. And such customs tend to persist surprisingly long times."

I was fascinated. I said, "I strongly suspect you are right."

The cleric smiled, "It is only speculation."

I shook my head in turn, replied, "But a very astute speculation." The cleric looked pleased at my praise, perhaps he had his share of vanity, but I meant what I said. We were moving again. Still only the two of us. I thought of something and said, "There is antagonism between the people of my parish and the adjoining parish. Brawls and occasional bloodshed occur. This seems connected with an attempt by the men of my parish to seize or capture part of the land of the adjoining parish. This has been going on a long time, I believe."

The cleric commented, "Parish boundaries were often set at boundaries of neighbouring tribes. And tribes tended to fight each other, so this is another example of a very long-lived custom or practice, continuing well after all memory of the original cause or circumstance had been lost."

I said, "I did not realize that. Of course there had to be some reason for putting parish boundaries where they are. This has been a most illuminating discussion. Thank you." We were at my stop and I rose, picked up my suitcase and shook hands with the man. I walked to my father's house, feeling I now understood the situation hereabouts much better.

Working for Potter now, I also better understood what he was doing and why he was doing it. But I was more and more seeing things in his professional behaviour I felt uneasy about. With two of his patients I felt his diagnoses were wrong. I tried to steer him to what I thought were the right diagnoses by asking questions, by being indirect, but hit a stone wall or rather a stone will. He wouldn't listen to my hints, seemed to resent them when he wasn't blandly dismissing my concerns. This left me in a quandary.

For once I was glad when the Holidays ended. I had been pleased to find the atmosphere in my father's and "stepmother's" house warm and affectionate. Both adults were much happier, my half-sister was growing rapidly, talking and walking, very inquisitive. I just hoped she stayed healthy enough to avoid Potter's ministrations. I told my "stepmother" about my opinions of Potter's competence, for I certainly didn't want my half-sister lost. She seemed the link of affection between my father and "stepmother" and I very much wanted that affection to continue.

The second term followed the pattern of the first, except my excursions with Miss Millen were now become a matter of custom. I had achieved the status of Miss Millen's "young man", a status rewarded by meals Sunday afternoons with her father and mother.

After, we were allowed to sit together on the sofa and talk. Just talk. Supervision was discrete but present.

Our conversations were about the play we had attended—still gratis seats—or the free public lecture we had heard or the free concert we had enjoyed. Miss Millen—Maud, I should say, for we were now on a first name basis—had definite opinions and a definite point of view. This prompted discussions. One of these occurred after we heard a modern play presented. The play was from the Norwegian playwright, Ibsen.

I found it utterly depressing: the central character, a woman, was trapped, trapped socially and intellectually and emotionally because of her sex. Yet I, once again, was led to think how trapped I was, how confined my path, because of the circumstances of my family. Leaving with Maud, I was reflecting on this and on how all of us were trapped, all on a march toward our deaths.

Maud interrupted this mordant reverie, asking me, "What did you think of the play?"

I replied, "It was very depressing. I confess I much prefer lighter fare." I had the feeling Maud had a commentary pent up and I had heard, in conversations with other students, that it was the gentlemanly thing to uncork such and stand clear. So I said, "What are your opinions?"

Maud told me, "The point of the play is that women are forced into a role they may not like by society, by social custom or expectations. This may produce unhappiness, possibly what is called hysteria or at times outright madness. I think this is true in this country, that women as a class are treated badly. We are not permitted our true nature but trapped into playing a role."

I thought about what she said. I knew what she was talking about; was that why my mother had deserted us? Yet my father's lot was hardly Elysium. Finally, I commented, "We all of us are forced into a role if you like. That is what society, any human society, does, I think. It compels us all to conform to certain standards of behaviour."

Maud seemed impatient, asked me, "Are there any women studying medicine with you?"

"No, not at London, at least not yet. Probably in a few years."

"Yet women who want to be doctors and could be good doctors cannot be admitted."

I reminded her, "I think the idea is to allow men these opportunities so they may earn enough to support a wife while she is bearing and rearing their children. Humans are still mammals and primates, after all, and the principal duty of any species is to reproduce itself." I thought the conversation was verging on the improper.

But Maud paid no attention to this, just objected, "But some women do not want to have children."

I thought some more and returned, "In other words, you are saying our society still places too much emphasis on keeping to the rules and not enough on permitting individual variation. But I think we are moving, slowly and haltingly perhaps to the ideal, which . . ." Here we were crossing a street and Maud had taken my arm, which pleased me, ". . . is to permit anyone, whatever their nature, to do as their individual talents and desires and push will allow."

Now Maud was thoughtful, but finally nodded and said, "I have to agree with that goal. It just seems to go so slowly."

We were nearly at her family's door. I said, "Perhaps in historical terms, on a time scale of centuries, it appears to be moving rapidly in that direction. But on a day to day or year to year basis, yes, it is slow indeed." We were looking at each other as I said this, and I felt relieved we seemed in agreement.

Returning, I understood that Maud imagined that becoming a doctor was my life's ambition, one I could pursue because I was a man. But I realized that I chose medicine partly by accident and partly in order to be more attractive to women. I was too embarrassed to reveal the latter goal to Maud. Some irony there, perhaps.

If my family had money, if money was no obstacle, what would I have done? I thought and decided that I would have gone to Oxford, read history and become . . . an archaeologist; that was it. But money was of course a severe limitation.

On the sofa together the following Sunday evening, we talked about professional matters, specifically my reservations about the care provided by Potter. We were turned toward each other, not exactly *tête a tête* but fairly close. I said, "I have been thinking about this situation some weeks, and I don't believe I can continue working for him, not in good conscience. I am well aware I am an utter tyro, venturing criticism of a man with decades of experience, but I have talked to practitioners here and am convinced I am right. All doctors on qualifying take an oath, called the Hippocratic Oath after a famous ancient Greek doctor. It begins, 'First, do no harm.' And that means, in my view, not knowingly allowing another doctor to do harm."

Maud asked, "How much has he been paying you?"

I answered, "Five shillings a week."

Maud said, "David, you should be able to make much more than that in London. If Potter asks, you just say you need to earn much more than he is paying you so you can qualify."

I nodded. After a short silence, I said, "In a sense I feel obligated to him, working all these years."

Maud shook her head and commented, "You earned every shilling I am sure. I doubt any of that money was in any sense a gift."

I said, "I asked him to write a letter recommending me for the scholarship. I did get the scholarship."

Maud asked, "Do you know that he wrote a letter?"

I was silent, and then said, "I don't know that for certain. I will inquire." I checked my watch, realized it was late, and apologized for keeping her up with my complaints.

As we stood up, she said, "I enjoy talking to you, David."

I replied, "And I with you." We smiled at each other and I took my leave. We had not progressed to displays of physical affection, even holding hands. I wondered if I was supposed to be more aggressive. One part of me definitely wanted to do this, another, my shy self, restrained me. And Maud's manner was not inviting of such.

I began canvassing for summer work. In this, I was in competition with some colleagues, but everyone seemed open and helpful. We were all in the same boat. Eventually I heard of a large apothecary shop that might hire me for the summer. I went there, talked to the proprietor, and apparently passed muster. He couldn't guarantee a job the full twelve weeks, but offered three pounds a week. I accepted. The job required fairly precise weighing of ingredients, making these into pills or preparing solutions at precise prescribed concentrations.

I also inquired as to who had recommended me for the scholarship. I was told the headmaster of the school and my Greek master; when I had told Potter I had gotten the scholarship, he seemed to be accepting of my praise and thanks. My opinion of Potter as a man fell significantly. I told Maud what I had discovered, and she merely nodded. She was pleased about the job. I suggested we might attend some concerts, actually paying for our seats, this summer. She seemed pleased at that as well.

As it happened, I worked at the apothecary nearly the entire twelve weeks. Aside from cheap seats at concerts and a play, I was able to find myself and still set aside over £30, which would help.

I had to return home. My main reason was the last £100 my father had promised me, but of course I felt I had to retain familial connections also. I arrived to find my half-sister Rose was very sick: she had a fever, one side of her face was swollen and I could feel swollen lymph nodes in her neck, indicating an infection. Her throat was very sore, according to my step-mother. Against my advice, she had gotten Potter to look at Rose and he had prescribed a medicine. The medicine, a liquid, was not helping. I sniffed the bottle and understood why.

I looked at my step-mother and shook my head. I turned Rose so the light from the window shone in Rose's face. Then I asked Rose to open her mouth so I could see inside it. After asking twice to open it wide, and turning Rose's head a little, I thought I could see something sticking out of one of Rose's tonsils. I asked my step-mother for tweezers, explaining that I needed them to pull out whatever it was, probably a small bone.

My step-mother found a pair of tweezers and I explained to Rose what I was going to do.

"Will it hurt?" she asked.

I said, "It hurts now, doesn't it? If I remove whatever it is, you will get better." Rose looked at my step-mother who nodded. So again Rose submitted to opening her mouth very wide, which itself was painful.

I spotted the "foreign body" and quickly grasped it with the tweezers and pulled it out. Rose shrieked. I looked at what I had removed. It was a small fish bone. I showed this to my step-mother, who was trying to comfort Rose. My stepmother said, "We had fish two days ago, and Rose began feeling poorly that night."

I said, "Give Rose broth, no solids, to drink. Also water." I spoke to Rose, "Sister, you had this lodged in your throat and it was making you sick. I am sorry I hurt you, but the fishbone had to come out. Now you will get better." I mentally knocked on wood as I said this.

Eventually I was able to get Rose to open her mouth again. I could see blood and pus draining from the tear I had made in the tonsil pulling the bone out. Unfortunately, with the swelling of the tonsil around the fishbone, it would probably have been impossible to remove the fishbone gently.

Rose was able to swallow warm broth, which should help rinse and calm the tonsil. I sat with her, occasionally gauging her temperature by touching her forehead, gently feeling the side of her face, once or twice looking into her mouth. The pain, the swelling, the fever all subsided over the next few hours. Rose was also able to sleep for the first time in two days, according to my step-mother. I was extremely anxious. Rose was in a sense my first patient and a near relation to boot.

My father seemed stolid through all this, yet I realized he had been anxious too. At one point he and my step-mother stood together, his arm about her shoulders, watching Rose and myself. I slept on a cot near Rose's crib, waking every five minutes it seemed to check on my half-sister, yet her recovery continued apace. The next morning she wanted to go outside and play, but I insisted she stay indoors at least another day to recover more fully.

At length I decided to take a walk. I was still on edge, fearing a relapse, but otherwise very pleased with myself. Early the next morning I set out. My route led me past the high meadow where my ancestors had lived, and the "good man's croft." Looking at the patch of untended wilderness squatting in its corner of the field, I thought I glimpsed Landrum's big bay horse in or near the croft. I wondered at that but continued on my walk. No birds.

Returning I found Landrum atop his bay horse standing in the lane. I got the impression he was waiting for me. Something winked in the sun: it was a camera hanging from his neck by a strap. I decided a friendly approach was best, and asked, "I say, Landrum, were you taking pictures in the 'good man's croft'?"

He stared at me, finally saying, "Now why should I do that?"

Something was amiss. His face looked strained and I felt uneasy. However, I elected to continue in a friendly fashion, so said, "On the train coming here I met a cleric who is also an antiquarian. I told him about the 'good man's croft' and he was quite interested, said he had not heard of one of those still existing, certainly this far south. He speculated that those patches went back to the introduction of farming in these Isles. He was going to contact some archaeologists to ask your parents if the archaeologists could examine the croft."

Landrum shifted in his saddle. I couldn't read anything from his expression save that my friendly approach was going nowhere. His horse stood nearly motionless.

At length he said, "I don't think my parents would want that."

I replied, "Well that is their choice." A pause, then I asked, "Are you still at Oxford?"

Landrum continued looking at me, finally said, "No. I have digs in London now."

I was becoming quite uneasy. I began to think he was trying to make up his mind about what to do about me, and was becoming aware that I might not care for some of the alternatives he was considering. It was almost as though he considered me to be some sort of threat. I moved sideways to the dry stone wall and picked one of the rocks off the top. I was prepared to throw it at his head if he rode at me. The wall was perhaps 4-5 feet high, enough to keep sheep confined, a little low to protect me if I jumped over it.

We were staring at each other when a woman's voice broke the silence: "There you are, Peter. Who is this?" Two young women riding side-saddle on smaller horses had come up behind Landrum.

He looked startled, then confused, and then composed his features as he turned toward the women. He smiled at them, said, "Lucille. Jane. This is an old school chum."

I was amazed he should refer to me in such a fashion, but set the rock back and touched my cap, saying, "Ladies."

The one who had spoken, a pretty, young, blonde woman, merely glanced at me, her interest was in Landrum. The other, whom I took to be a kind of chaperone-companion, was not as pretty though about the same age. She gave me more of her attention, though I clearly was not considered suitable for purposes of conversation. The prettier one said, "We will be late for breakfast unless we hurry. We were hoping you could take some pictures of us. Your mother said you develop your own pictures." This as the three of them moved away down the lane, leaving me alone.

Landrum didn't look back as he rode next the prettier woman and the three of them were soon out of sight. I walked quickly back to my father's house, shaken. What was going on?

Rose was playing with a doll in the house. I looked at her throat, was amazed at how quickly she had recovered; the lymph nodes were normal or nearly so and her temperature felt normal too. She had forgiven me for the pain I had inflicted on her, which relieved me. I once more told my father and step-mother that while Potter could deal with most things, he had overlooked the obvious cause of Rose's illness, and the medicine he had provided probably made Rose's condition worse. However, it was best not to tell Potter that, as I wanted to stay on good terms with him. They nodded. My father gave me the rest of the money. I told them, "If I possibly can, I will repay the £300."

So I returned to London for my fourth year, my second of rounds. I was to pursue my fourth and fifth years of study in the new University College Hospital. This had officially opened in 1906, about three years before I started at University. The building was shaped like an X, with squared ends resembling turrets. I would have to pay about the same for fees, about the same for food, nothing for shelter and I had paid for the equipment and tools, the cadaver for example, so my overall expenses would be less. Still, paying for the fifth year was a nagging concern.

With the £30 from working over the summer for the apothecary, I had about £140 which would pay—just—for my fourth year. I was now a "clerk", assigned a number of patients to look after. I had to talk to each of them, obtain their symptoms, describe these, "present" them to a physician or group of physicians, and attempt to put a name to their condition along with a treatment. The physician or physicians would ask me questions, forcing me to defend my diagnoses, forcing me to think about the patients' illnesses. This was always anxious, occasionally humiliating, yet all in all a most useful and valuable training. I quickly learned to obtain as much information as possible about the patient, such as previous illnesses and occupations, and above all, to listen to the patient.

The men we followed on rounds were undoubtedly clever and accomplished, otherwise a mixed lot. Presentations of patients for some were a humiliating ordeal, designedly so, we all thought. Others we liked. Batty Shaw especially was very friendly and easy-going, considerate to patients and students alike. We would do our best for him. Not out of fear but from affection.

The patients we saw were mostly working class; labourers, craftsmen or clerks. The women were housewives, maids or servants. This was not surprising as the Hospital lay in the middle of a slum. Patients, children especially, often came to us in a moribund condition. I was told there were streets in the vicinity where constables wouldn't venture, even in pairs. Curiously though, nurses from the Hospital regularly visited patients throughout the area without fear of molestation. Still, I was very happy to be living in the Hospital rather than renting a room in the neighbourhood.

Presentations and rounds engrossed my time and nearly all my energy. Excursions to free events with Maud were my only diversion. I kept my expenses under rigid control. My medical equipment was second hand and so cheaper but still functional. Always the prospect of trying to find the money, over £100, for my last year lay at the back of my thoughts.

I continued my courtship of Maud, clearly with her parents' approval. I couldn't decide if this was with Maud's approval or not. She was not physically demonstrative of affection. Either she was physically cold or, more likely, was carefully rationing such demonstrations until my professional future was more secure. Either way, her behaviour seemed disconcertingly cold-blooded.

In one respect, I gained in intimacy with her. As a medical student, I was learning a great deal about the sexual and gynaecological aspects of women. This was both arousing and putting off. The clear message, repeated each day and often several times during each day, was that we were all animals, each with animal needs. This conflicted with the "angel of the house" ideals I had imbibed, grossly conflicted with them, yet . . . . Perhaps some compromise could be made, but exactly what would the terms be? Perhaps each couple had to work these out together.

Still, I was aware that Maud, like all human beings, had to eliminate, to empty bowels and bladder at intervals. As a woman, she also experienced a menstrual flow. On a few occasions, I noticed slight changes in her complexion, small facial spots appearing and then disappearing. This was accompanied by irritability and a reluctance to attend concerts, etc. On considering this, I realized there was a monthly recurrence of these symptoms and guessed the cause. So I adjusted the timing of my invitations.

Otherwise I was now a regular guest at her parents' house for Sunday dinners. Since the meals were much better than I could expect at the hospital, such a change in fare was most welcome. After the meal, Maud and I would sit on the sofa and talk. The vigilance of her parents was relaxed but unfortunately was unnecessary as Maud kept sufficient distance between us.

Our conversations revolved around what we had seen and done together, issues such as women's suffrage, Ireland, my experiences on rounds, my efforts to secure employment next summer and even occasional vague references to my/our future. I had told Maud of my anxiety, relief, and pride when I had cured my half-sister of what would almost certainly have been a fatal condition. I couldn't tell if she understood my feelings or not, but she listened.

I also described my encounters with Landrum and my vague suspicions about his behaviour. Here Maud seemed more interested, at one point asking me what Landrum looked like. This brought me to a full stop: I understood what she meant, yet I never thought of men in such terms. I had to describe him in relation to me, about the same height and build, brown hair like mine. I thought his eyes were blue as were mine . . .

Maud observed, "You speak of him as your twin."

I protested, "We are quite different looking. It is just hard for me to paint a picture of a man in words. You I can describe, but that is because I spend so much time looking at you and" here I coughed, finally finished, "thinking about you."

I fell silent, wondering if I had said too much, but Maud smiled, said, "Your studies seem to leave you with a great deal of time for thought, then."

I replied, assuming an air of gallantry, "Not nearly as much as I wish." She again smiled, and I realized Maud was at least happy I fancied her. We then proceeded to talk of other things.

As the term proceeded, I continued my efforts to secure summer employment, make that remunerative summer employment. I was able to make a couple of pounds working on odd days at the apothecary shop, days when for one reason or another rounds were cancelled. This money was spent mostly on Maud's (and my) entertainment, and on presents such as spirits for Maud's family in acknowledgement of the meals I had eaten there.

I continued to wonder about Maud's feelings for me. She clearly did not wear her heart on her sleeve if she did care for me. The only clue on this subject occurred after a concert we attended together. Maud had gone to the loo after the concert, leaving me waiting for her. I saw two female University students I knew slightly. We exchanged greetings and were talking about the concert when Maud returned. I introduced the three women, mentioning that the two other women were University students as well. Maud proceeded to pick two or three pieces of lint or loose threads from my coat in what I think the rest of us recognized as a proprietary gesture. Then I walked back with Maud to her home for dinner. I was now more confident of her, and on taking my leave that evening, I took her hand and kissed it. She accepted this; we then exchanged smiles and I departed.

My principal task as a medical student was of course to learn as much about medicine as I could. I listened closely to the staff doctors I was following on rounds. I asked questions to the limits of the tolerance of these men—there were no women doctors among them—sometimes took notes on what I had seen or heard and attended every lecture, again taking notes. My reading of the medical journals was more restricted, as I lacked the knowledge to follow many of the articles. Still, I persisted.

On my return home during the Holidays, I brought my medical instruments, hoping they would not be required. Rose was healthy, I was relieved to see. She had indeed forgiven me for the pain I had inflicted on her. Potter sent a note, requesting my services as deliverer of medicines. Unfortunately I was paid the same salary. I saw nothing of Landrum. His behaviour worried me enough that I carried one of my father's heavy walking sticks everywhere I went. The good man's croft looked even more sinister, but that must have been my imagination.

Just before I returned to London, my father asked me how much money I had and how much more I would need. I told him. He and my step-mother looked at each other and I guessed they had discussed this before I had arrived. My father said, "I have put by £50 more and can let you have that."

I was surprised, delighted at first, and then humbled. I told them, "That will get me almost through the first term of my last year. I really don't know what I can do for the second, but if I have to stay out a year working to earn money, then I will do that. But I will complete my course of studies and qualify." So I returned to London feeling hopeful.

SUNSHINE WITH CLOUDS

During my fourth term on rounds, I stepped up my campaign to secure summer employment. The money I would have at term's end would just not be enough, even if I could work the entire summer at the apothecary. Then one of my fellow students suggested I talk to a staff doctor who had a profitable side line: attesting recruits into a number of regiments of H. M.'s Army. The staff doctor hired students who had finished their fourth year to give medical examinations to recruits. For each recruit attested the doctor received 2/6, half a crown. He pocketed one shilling, leaving 1/6 for the student. If recruiting was brisk, I could expect to make perhaps a pound a day, though a very long day. Also, I would become a paid practitioner, and be learning my trade into the bargain.

The doctor didn't seem to have any other candidates for the job, so I was engaged. I was able to spend some time with him while he examined potential recruits to learn exactly what I needed to be measuring. He had me perform some examinations under his supervision until I was confident I could do the job. The only potential problem was a possible dearth of recruits, but the doctor was examining recruits for many regiments, some based in London, and he assured me there would be plenty of business. And that was what I wanted.

Maud and her family were pleased to hear of my new job, Maud particularly. At this point, I realized she wanted me to succeed, to qualify. Either she sympathized with my dreams or expected and desired to become the wife of a doctor. I could get no hint of what her true feelings were. This was unsettling yet kept me returning to be with her. And I kept returning to dine Sundays with her and her parents.

I wrote to my father and step-mother and to Potter informing them of my plans for the summer. My father wished me luck; Potter did not reply. In fact, on a few days without rounds, I was able to examine recruits, clearing over a pound before end of term. This was cheering.

The examinations themselves took place in a rather dark, shabby room with scales and an eye chart, etc. At first the staff doctor was there to supervise, but shortly left me on my own. Mostly I had to pay attention to details; some regiments had height requirements: they wanted to fill their ranks with tall men. All had minimum heights, but I had been told to pass the recruits if they were close to the minimum. Some put things in their shoes to improve their chances. I measured chest sizes, deflated and inflated, listened to their hearts, looked at their teeth to be sure they could eat Army rations, checked their eyesight, looked for hernias, and measured their weights. I had also been told I could pass obviously undernourished men as a few months of drill and regular meals would set them right. I would initial each man's document and the staff doctor would sign them. The Army would pay him and he would pay me.

After term ended, I began work six days a week. When no one was waiting to be examined, I would read medical journals. Business was quite variable, as few as ten or so prospective recruits in a day, as many as twenty five or more. With practice, I became more efficient. I also began to be able to see right away if a particular recruit wouldn't qualify or at best have problems. I was glad I was paid the same whether the recruit was acceptable or not.

A rush of men near the end of my first month brought me just under £25. With what I had saved and what my father had given me, I now had more than enough for the first, my penultimate, term; and I was within sight of paying for the second. My goal was nearly attained. In recognition of this news, Maud again allowed me to hold her hand and kiss it.

Just above £30 my second month and I had what I needed, and possibly something over. There was a jewellery shop near where I worked and I decided to get Maud something, as I was feeling vastly better about my prospects. So one slow morning, I went over to the place and looked and looked. I kept returning to the store over the afternoon and finally decided on a broach. The store was also a pawn shop and I guessed the broach hadn't been redeemed.

It was a flower: I think a daisy, apparently in silver with gold fill. It looked authentic. It certainly cost authentic. I paid 10 shillings, which seemed a lot but I wanted to show Maud I valued her. And I was happy, relieved, the lowering cloud of worry about money now lifting. I had a future, one I was beginning to hope she would be willing to share.

Accordingly, on the next slow day I went to the Millens' shop. Mr Millen was there behind the counter. I asked for Maud and he called for her, saying, "Your young man is here," winking at me. Maud had been doing the books and I noted signs of her menstrual courses on her face. She seemed irritated at my calling then, but her courses did make her irritable.

I apologized for interrupting her and handed her the box with the broach, saying, "This is for you." I smiled at her and left.

My invitations for Sunday meals were now understood: a matter of routine. This Sunday, I brought a bottle of gin, a good quality gin; as that was what the Millens drank. They were welcoming as always, yet the parents often glanced at their daughter, who often glanced at me. Something was in the offing. I noticed Maud was wearing the broach, which reassured me. I was afraid such a gift might seem a little forward.

The meal dispatched, Maud and I adjourned once more to the sofa. I told her of a play, a revival of *The Importance of Being Earnest* by Wilde; and she readily agreed to accompany me, saying she had heard of the play and very much wanted to see it.

Then she said, "Thank you very much for the broach, David. I apologize for my irritation when you brought it to our shop, but there was a muddle in the books that vexed me."

I replied, "You are welcome. I hope you dissolved the muddle."

Maud nodded, hesitated, and finally said, "I hope this doesn't offend you, but Father and Mother had the broach appraised. They were told it was genuine."

I was surprised but said, "I would have been vastly more offended if it were fake. No, I am not offended, I am relieved. And am very happy you are wearing it."

Maud said, "The fact is, they thought it was meant as a betrothal gift."

I was startled. Maud was clearly expecting me to explain myself. So were her parents, I was sure. In truth, I wanted to express my happiness by making her happy. However, I knew she was asking a serious question and expected a serious reply. So I said, "I wanted to please you because I esteem you. I have to acknowledge I may have been premature in giving you that broach. You know of my situation. I hope to be able to make a reasonable living and . . ." here I cleared my throat as I was very nervous, "and I had hoped . . ." I swallowed and finally was able to say, "I had hoped you would share my portion. I mean, as my wife."

I fell silent. I was very hot, very embarrassed, beginning to wilt. But I had said what I meant. Maud looked at me and smiled. Her eyes sparkled. I was going to tell her she needn't reply right away when she said, "David, I accept your proposal of marriage. Of course, we will have to wait until you are established, but that shouldn't take more than a year or two."

I commented, "I sincerely hope not." Here I was able to return her smile.

We were smiling at each other when a magical thing happened: I realized she expected me to kiss her, a kiss of betrothal. I leaned forward as did she and we kissed each other on the lips. Several times, in fact. For good measure I kissed her on her cheek and her throat, then on her lips again. This was arousing to me and I thought she looked a little flushed. We moved together on the sofa and I put my arm across her shoulders and we kissed some more. We eventually had both our arms about each other for good measure.

Something occurred to me and I asked Maud, "I suppose I should ask your parents' permission."

Maud shook her head and replied, "You already have their approval. They like you. They will be very pleased when I tell them."

I asked, "But what are your feelings on the subject?"

For answer, she kissed me again, a lingering kiss with a slightly opened mouth. This was more arousing; I hoped I wouldn't embarrass myself when I had to stand up.

To distract myself, I told Maud, "Once I am paid for this month's work, I should have enough for us to attend a much wider range of events."

Maud said, "I will enjoy that, I am sure, but you must be certain you have enough to qualify. That is most important."

I nodded, and then noting the time, took my leave. We embraced and kissed before I left, my (and her) fate being settled.

Business was reasonably good the last month of summer: I pocketed over £25, almost £80 in all, leaving me with a cushion, uniquely in my experience. And of course instead of a "best girl" I had a fiancée. Two uncertainties were now removed. We attended Wilde's play along with two concerts and began talking about personal things: children and my dress. Maud didn't want to have children until we could afford it, and I agreed. And she felt I needed a tailor-made suit of clothes, rather than the second-hand regalia I had purchased in her father's shop. She said I needed to look like a doctor rather than a medical student.

I nodded, and after some silence I said, "I will ask my colleagues where I should get what is necessary and have the measurements made the first open day." So we were once again in agreement.

As Maud had stated, her parents were pleased to have me join their family. I wrote to my father and step-mother with the news, both financial and matrimonial. I wanted to introduce Maud to my family, but space for sleeping was a problem. Eventually we had photographs made as the next best alternative. This was after I had obtained my new clothes, so was able to wear them for the photograph. Maud said I looked very professional.

As the term proceeded, I could substitute occasionally for the staff doctor to make a few "bob". I would spend these on Maud, now I could escort her to places in the evenings. Concerts, plays, dining at moderately expensive restaurants consumed any extra monies I had. It was enjoyable doing these things with her, even more enjoyable kissing and fondling each other afterwards, still with limits which I accepted.

Near end of term, we attended an opera together, Massenet's *Manon*, good singing to be sure yet a depressing story. Afterwards we went out in the entrance hall heading for the door when I saw Landrum. He was escorting a young woman; not the one who was visiting a year or so ago, and unfortunately he saw me.

"Ah, Mendy," he said.

I replied, "Landrum."

He seemed taken with Maud, spoke to his companion, an attractive, expensively dressed woman, turned to me and said, "I think introductions are in order. This is Miss Felicity Turner. David Mendy and I were in school together."

I was again surprised he should have the face to mention our association in school, but had to reply, "May I present my fiancée, Miss Maud Millen. Lord Peter Landrum."

Maud was staring at Landrum, quite transfixed. This annoyed Landrum's companion, quite irritated me, yet looking at Landrum, I realized he was quite handsome. I noticed several other women looking admiringly at him.

My enemy and my fiancée looked at each other until Landrum's companion said, "Do let us go, Peter. We are expected." To me, she said, "A pleasure meeting you," as she pulled at Landrum's arm. I gathered the pleasure was reserved to me, as opposed to Maud.

They moved off, Maud continuing to gaze at Landrum until he and his companion disappeared. Maud did not take my arm as we followed, further angering me. We walked until it started to rain, when I secured a taxi. This was an expensive evening in more ways than one.

I was silent. I couldn't think of anything to say that wouldn't precipitate a public quarrel. On arrival at her home, I paid the driver. I had to escort her to her door rather than immediately take the taxi back to the hospital, and I was thinking of the extra cost. The rain had stopped. We stood looking at each other at her door. I was about to tell her, "Goodnight" and leave when she apparently realized I was upset.

"David, what is the matter?"

"That is for you to tell me."

Again we stared at each other. For a moment I thought she was going to make fun of me, of my feelings, but finally she said, "I offended you, made you jealous. I admit I found him to be quite good looking. You didn't tell me he was so handsome."

I forced myself to be civil: "I just don't think of men in such ways. The woman he was with didn't like his behaviour either. Or yours."

Silence again while Maud digested this. Once more I felt she was going to say something angry, sarcastic, but again she realized that would make a strained situation worse. At length she said, "Then I apologize for hurting your feelings. It was unintentional and thoughtless. Please forgive me."

My resentment, my jealousy melted. I was contrite, ashamed of myself. I bent forward and kissed her, and then said, "I will accept your apology if you will accept mine for," I searched for an appropriate description of my behaviour, "my churlishness. If it were any other man, I wouldn't have minded a fraction as much." I decided a compliment was in order, and added, "I will just have to get used to other men ogling my very pretty fiancée."

Maud reached up and kissed me again. She said, "Come inside, David." We hung our coats up and sat down on the sofa. Maud asked me, "Why do you fear and dislike him so much?"

I was surprised at her question. I replied, "I will describe him as I knew him, but be warned: what I will be telling you is probably not the sort of story a gentleman should be telling a lady." I gave her a chance to demur, but she did not. I went on, "He was monitor of one of the houses in the grammar school I attended. He was three years ahead of me. I was in a different house. The houses compete against each other in games and I soon realized Landrum had to be watched. He went out of his way to injure, to hit or kick me. I do not know why. However, he had the services of a fag, a very young looking boy. I and the other boys I dined with were convinced that some of the services provided were of a . . ." I hesitated, cleared my throat and forced out, ". . . sexual nature."

I paused to give Maud a chance to object to my continuing but she did not. I said, "We all also got the impression the boy did not like what was being done to him. After the Holidays, the boy didn't return. Then we were told the boy had killed himself. That is fact. There were rumours of a suicide note that named Landrum as the cause of the boy's despair. However, it is also a fact that Landrum was sent down, despite being a house monitor, in the last term of his last year. Whatever he did was clearly regarded as extremely serious by the headmaster and the governors of the school. So he never graduated the school, and why he calls me a school chum baffles me."

I fell silent. Maud shook her head. "What a terrible story," she said.

"I agree. And yet everyone else in the school knew what I am telling you, so why he has seemed so threatening to me on the few occasions we have met when I was home is beyond me. At least he has good taste in women," I smiled at her as I said this. She smiled back; we moved together, embraced and kissed as had become our custom.

Returning, I reflected on the evening. Our differences had been resolved without quarrelling. Maud was paying attention to me and wanted our relationship to continue. I felt the same way, so in a sense our intimacy had advanced and deepened, which was good. Yet I feared that Landrum would begin to pursue Maud and I could not be certain of her constancy, given Landrum's advantages of appearance, manners and fortune. Was he genuinely attracted to her or was he rather trying to hurt me? He really did seem interested in her . . . I simply didn't know. I could not imagine him wanting to marry Maud nor could I imagine Maud's family countenancing his pursuit. On that thought, I retired to my cot under a stairwell.

End of term was nearing and Maud began to suggest she wanted to visit my family: she felt they should meet her. Fair enough, though the suspicion that she wanted to see the Landrum estate crossed my mind. However, I agreed. We would have to leave very early and return very late. I bought an alarm clock in aid of this project.

Although I disliked early risings, the trip itself was rather fun. I liked travelling with Maud and I think she was enjoying the expedition also. She seemed interested in the area and I told her about the antagonism between the parishes and about the good man's croft. She was very surprised at the persistence of what had to be very old practices.

On the walk to my father's house I commented:

"It is surprising, here in A. D. 1913 England, and of course untestable. But, it explains a lot. For example, I have always been able to tell which parish anyone in this area comes from, based on their accents and speech patterns. They just do not mix."

We reached the house and were welcomed by my father, step-mother and half-sister. Rose was growing fast: she was actually approaching Maud's height. My step-mother praised Maud's beauty; my father was clearly very impressed as well. We were asked about our plans. Maud said, "David has to qualify, then get a job. Children will have to be supported, so David's earnings will decide when and how many."

My step-mother asked, "So you will be giving up your bookkeeping?"

Maud answered, "I think so. I would like to get away from London, but we will have to see what David is offered."

I said, "Which is impossible to predict. But, for now, at least the road to qualification is open."

Since we had to leave fairly soon after arrival, there wasn't much else we could do. I was irritated by Maud's interest in seeing the Landrum house. I said, "The house can't be seen from the road and the family doesn't welcome uninvited strangers." So we returned, I somewhat unsettled by her proposal. She appeared to sense this, holding my hand as if to reassure me.

I managed to collect a pound or two over the Holidays attesting recruits. This I spent on Maud, taking her dining at two disconcertingly expensive, yet not very good, restaurants. Maud agreed the food wasn't worth the charges but she said she enjoyed dining at these places, so I was happy to be the provider of the experiences. Aside from that, we took walks and talked and, again within limits, fondled each other. I was becoming increasingly impatient, wanting to take her to bed. The curse of Adam was fully mine.

My last term was busier, due to the men I was following on rounds, so I wasn't able to make as much at my second job. Maud and I attended several concerts, an opera and a ballet, all very enjoyable, particularly to Maud, who was attracting attention from other men. Again, I had mixed feelings about this, but since we didn't see Landrum, I held my peace.

To obtain the M. B. and qualify, I had to pass the qualifying exam. We were assured this exam was rigorous, that it was possible to fail it, that we had to take it seriously. This I did, increasing my review of the material in the lectures. My notes from these were by now quite extensive. Otherwise I spent the time mainly worrying. Maud did her best to encourage and reassure me, which helped.

The exam was indeed extensive: we had to write papers on clinical subjects, undergo a *viva voce* quizzing by outside doctors, and examine a patient under their scrutiny. I actually felt I had done well, but tried to suppress feelings of satisfaction, believing a worried attitude was less likely to be unlucky. My precautions were sufficient, as it turned out: I was told I had passed.

DAVID MENDY, M. B.

Qualified at last. I still had some money and bought Maud a pearl necklace, to which she responded by permitting greater physical intimacy and agreeing to consider marriage as soon as I could come up with money for a honeymoon. We tentatively decided on the end of summer as a target.

In the meantime, I was now able to attest recruits on my own, and the staff doctor who had sponsored me agreed to let me take over what had been his pitch. Business was as erratic as before but I was confident of amassing at least £75 or so this summer, enough for Maud and me to start our life together. Maud's parents were agreeable to me living with them, so while I would contribute something towards their rent and food, Maud and I could start accumulating money to buy a practice or part of one.

I became aware that events on the Continent were encroaching on British consciousness. War between the European great powers was becoming a probability, and Britain's becoming involved was a growing possibility. Though I personally would benefit from expansion of the Army, the prospect of our Army becoming part of the fighting was appalling.

Maud's brother was between voyages, and we met. He was now qualified as a first mate. He was nearly as tall as I, bluff and brown, with blue eyes, very like his father. I wondered how Maud's and my children would turn out, assuming we had any. He seemed to approve of me as a brother-in-law, and so I became friendly with him. Over dinner, the possibility of war with Germany and Austria-Hungary was a topic that rapidly engrossed our time together. I was now dining there nearly every evening and could feel Maud's family opinion shifting toward British participation, especially if the Germans invaded Belgium. We agreed they would be foolish, criminally foolish, to do so, yet rationality seemed to be ebbing everywhere.

The axe fell 4 August, 1914; within days, I was working twelve, then fourteen hours a day. Once again, my meals were out of tins, unheated, eaten standing, though I could afford beef stew as often as I wished. The staff doctor I had substituted for returned, several other doctors began working also, yet the queues of recruits grew and grew. The staff doctor I had replaced confided to me that he had been hoping to confine his attentions to his practice, yet the combined lures of patriotic, professional duty and the money to be made had ensnared him and the rest of us.

Like the others, I insisted on one day off a week. For me this was Sunday. Maud's brother got a ship and left. After dinner, Maud and I would discuss our prospects. We agreed I needed to continue working even though I was making enough for a full-scale honeymoon at a reasonably posh place nearly every day. In fact, I would be able to repay my father with interest and the purchase of a practice was becoming an increasingly realistic prospect.

The only problem we could see would be when the rush of recruits eased. At this point, I would be expected to join the Army Medical Corps myself. This would separate us for months at a time, which I didn't like at all, but what else could we do? I wouldn't have a practice myself, and doctors would be needed to deal with casualties. I confessed to Maud that I was apprehensive about having to treat wounded men, some badly wounded. Mistakes on my part could cost some of our volunteers their lives. Maud nodded. I felt she understood my uncertainties.

At work, I was struck time and again by the greater physical fitness of the "Kitchener volunteers" compared to the pre-war men. As I mentioned to Maud, this also spoke volumes about social conditions in Britain. Instead of the sweepings of the slums, men enlisting for the prospect of regular meals, we were seeing mostly the middle and even upper-middle classes.

Summer passed into fall, then into winter. Mercifully, the queues became shorter as vast numbers of men were incorporated into battalions of volunteers. I could not believe the amounts of money I was getting. I showed the cheques to Maud, who was also amazed and delighted. I opened a banker's account. One Sunday during the Holidays, Maud and I again visited my family, this time bearing £400, repayment of my father's generous support with interest. I told my father, "I suppose this makes me a war profiteer, but please accept this with my gratitude and thanks." I thought my father and step-mother were touched by my words. I told Rose the money was her dowry.

As spring approached the recruiting business was definitely ebbing. On the other hand, the hospitals were overwhelmed with casualties. So I arranged with another staff doctor to alternate days examining recruits. I went to Charing Cross Hospital to work as a volunteer on the off days. If I was going to be an Army doctor treating wounded men, I wanted to have as much experience as possible.

Maud approved of this arrangement. However, I was becoming more anxious about her setting a day for our marriage. I felt we had enough money, now over £1,000, put by. She seemed hesitant and I began to wonder what was going on. Her parents were a little embarrassed, shifty-eyed, or so I imagined. Was Landrum seeing her in secret? I remembered a question she had asked my father and step-mother on our last visit, about recruiting. My father said there were plenty of volunteers but the situation was complicated by the antagonism between the parishes. I now suspected she was fishing for information about Landrum who of course would be one of the officers. In an officer's uniform, he would cut an even more dashing figure.

So I began to sulk. Maud noticed this, and one evening I broached the question of marriage, asking her if she was having second thoughts or was hesitant for other reasons. She looked away, was silent a considerable time, and finally said:

"We can marry whenever you wish, David. You have been so busy, that I thought it had slipped your mind. You are very focused on your training, as you call it."

At this, we both fell silent. Finally I told her:

"Maud, perhaps this is just my imagination, perhaps my suspicions are unworthy ones, but I have never really been confident of your affections. I keep noticing a certain absence of mind, as though your thoughts were engrossed by someone else, and you simply haven't been enthusiastic about our union. If you want our engagement to marry to end, please say so. We must be open and candid with each other."

More silence until Maud said:

"David, I accepted your proposal of marriage and haven't changed my mind. I admit I was fascinated by your former schoolmate, but any absence of mind has other origins, worry about my brother especially. I will marry you whenever you wish."

I thought, and said, "Let us say two weeks from today, then. I will make arrangements for my replacement. Where do you want to honeymoon?"

This time the silence lasted so long I thought Maud was really going to throw me over. However she finally said, "I think the West Country, Cornwall and Devon. Lorna Doone country."

I smiled, greatly relieved. We had both liked that book. I said, "The West Country it will be. Two weeks of honeymoon, let us say. Or more if you wish. I will move my things here beforehand, then we can marry and go. Would a Registry Office wedding do?"

Maud nodded. I hoped for some enthusiasm, but acquiescence seemed all I was going to get. Still, the thing was settled at last. Or was it?

I returned to the hospital, lay my bedding on the derelict sofa under a stairwell where I slept, removed my shoes and outer clothing and lay down. I had no blanket but it was warm enough. I lay thinking about love. I was aware people married for all sorts of reasons, silly, selfish, mercenary reasons sometimes but like most people, I hoped for true affection between my spouse and myself. A union of spirits, of souls. Closeness, companionship. Was I being naïve?

My thoughts turned back to my last term as a student. One day, a fellow student commented that a woman admitted with symptoms of appendicitis said her name was Mendy. Since I knew of no relations bearing my name, I went to talk to the woman. She didn't seem to be in much pain and I asked about her symptoms, all very routine, until I said, "Mendy is an unusual name. It is my name. I am David Mendy."

She stared at me, finally saying, "David."

I exhaled and managed to reply, "Mother."

We looked at each other, both began to speak, she quieted and I took the floor:

"I am a few weeks from qualifying as a doctor. I have a fiancée. I don't know when we will marry. Mother, why did you leave us?"

I saw she had tears in her eyes. She looked up at me and spoke, "I married your father to have a home, an establishment, but I really couldn't stand the idea of living out my life there with him. There was nothing really wrong with your father, but I just felt so hemmed in, so confined, I had to leave. I am very happy to have a doctor as a son. I am sure your fiancée loves you and that you will make her happy."

I asked, "What do you do for a living, Mother?"

She looked away, and then said, "I am housekeeper for a solicitor. I won't tell you his name. I am happy there. How is your father?"

I replied, "Father remarried. I think he and my step-mother are happy together. I believe they love each other. They have a daughter, my half-sister Rose."

My mother was silent until, "It would be best if you not tell him about me. There is no point in opening old wounds. It is good he found someone."

I nodded, smiled and said, "I have wondered about you over the years. If you want to write to me, you can send the letter to the hospital and I will get it. I will leave you to rest and recover."

I bent down and kissed her on her cheek, very unprofessional of course, but my mother smiled.

Afterwards I thought about my mother's life. I guessed she was probably the mistress of the man whose servant she was, evidently her choice. She apparently found marriage too confining, which confused me. I thought women wanted a husband just as most men wanted a wife, but my mother was exceptional. She would probably be in her forties, yet she was still attractive.

I had talked to Maud afterwards about meeting my mother and about the life my mother preferred. Maud commented that some women did indeed not want to be confined in a marriage, but noting my change of expression, said she was not one of them. This had reassured me at the time, but now, remembering, I wondered yet again about Maud's true feelings for me.

I spent the early part of our wedding day moving my things to the Millens' flat. Maud's father and mother seemed happy to have me living with them, and it would certainly save on rent. Maud investigated hotels where we would be staying and picked one. I acquiesced; it was her honeymoon after all.

I had talked to married colleagues about sex. I was a virgin as presumably was Maud. I knew a great deal about various aspects of the subject, but my knowledge was all theoretical. One of the staff doctors, a man in his forties, gave me what I was sure was good advice: "Mendy, don't be in a hurry. Take your time. Let her set the pace." I nodded and hoped I could follow it. Perhaps the novelty of the situation would put me off enough. I did want to give her pleasure, both to ensure she would want to repeat the experience and because I loved her. I would use condoms, another unfamiliar technique, also tending to slow my completion. Or so I had been advised.

Otherwise, I was very happy to get away from the hospital. I was certainly learning a great deal about treating wounded men. I was also humbled by their bravery and stoicism, enduring pain from often awful wounds. Of course, these were the men who had survived what had befallen them. I began to understand that sooner was better when it came to treating casualties. I could only hope and pray I would be able to meet the challenges of dealing with repeated medical emergencies. The stress of even relatively diluted service, always under some sort of supervision, was producing more frequent nightmares. I felt ashamed of these, so didn't tell Maud about them. The tension in the hospital was building as rumours gathered of another offensive, with the attendant swamp of hospital facilities. For this reason also I was glad to get away.

MARRIAGE

On our way to the Registry office, I urged a detour to buy a ring. This proved difficult owing to the thinness of Maud's fingers. There was a ring she liked which was too big, so I bought another ring of the correct size and also paid for the ring she liked to be sized for her. She would be able to wear that ring when we returned from the honeymoon.

Once married, we went back to the Millens for our baggage, one suitcase each, and headed for the train station we wanted. We went by taxi to avoid comments by women who felt I should be in uniform. Unhappily, there were two women in our compartment who felt the same way. Maud came to my defence, telling the women I was working as a volunteer at Charing Cross hospital and would be joining the Army Medical Corps after returning from our honeymoon. This quieted my critics.

We reached our destination after nightfall. The hotel was in walking distance from the train station and we arrived there in full darkness. I wanted a room with its own bathroom, but the hotel didn't provide those. I paid for a week, collected the key and we took our suitcases to the room ourselves. I opened the door, turned to my wife and gathered her in my arms. I carried her across the threshold and sat her down inside. We kissed.

Maud seemed nervous; I was definitely nervous, but was not going to admit this to her. She said, "I think the hotel restaurant is still serving. I am hungry."

So I replied, "Let us leave the suitcases here and get something to eat."

We were able to get sandwiches and beer. It was a rather tense meal. We returned to our room. We opened our suitcases and proceeded to change into night wear. I was increasingly aroused and increasingly embarrassed. We kept glancing at each other. Watching Maud's successive removal of her dress, chemise, stockings, etc. was most entertaining. I don't know how she felt as I removed my clothing but she certainly seemed interested. She turned her back for removal of her penultimate item of clothing, enabling me to remove my drawers and put on my nightshirt. I had purchased that for this occasion, as I normally slept in drawers and stockings. Maud then disappointed me by putting on her nightgown before pulling off her drawers. I took a condom out of its package, raised the nightshirt and put the condom on according to the instructions I had gotten from more knowledgeable colleagues. Maud watched, increasing my embarrassment. We got into the bed together.

I told my bride, "Let me know if you like what I will be doing to you or if you don't. I want to make this and every time we lie together as pleasant for you as possible."

I accompanied these words with fondling her breasts. These were on the small side, yet Maud said, "I am enjoying what you are doing."

I could feel the points of her nipples through the cloth of her nightgown. I wanted to suck on them, but had to content myself with kissing them through the cloth, also well received. While doing this, I began caressing up her nightgown. I had been told what place to rub or rather caress and did so.

Maud said, "That feels very good, David. Continue."

I did so, noting she was breathing faster, until she began to groan and shudder. I guessed I had satisfied her but now urgently wanted satisfaction myself. So I pushed her legs apart, knelt between them and pulled up my nightshirt.

I had been warned that sexual intercourse was an awkward business at first. I pushed my rubber-clad penis where I thought her vagina was, heard Maud say, "A little higher, David," raised my "member" and felt something give way in Maud. I entered her smoothness, pulled back, pushed in again, and again and again, feeling both increasing pleasure and pressure. Then both ebbed, and I realized my seed had escaped. I lay upon my bride, now my wife, until my penis softened and fell out of her. I kissed her; we held each other until I rolled off her. I needed to wash out the condom, and did that in one of the bathrooms near our room. I hung the thing upside down in the closet after washing it.

Maud asked, "When will we do that again?"

I said, "You have disarmed me," pointing to my groin, "but my spirits will revive, given my pretty bride." We kissed again, and then slept.

Over the next few days, we lived in our own world, having sex almost as often as I could manage, sleeping late, and eating at all hours. Otherwise, we walked together, hand in hand or arm in arm, enjoying the views of the sea, the cliffs, beaches and hills rising inland. Many other couples were honeymooning there or just enjoying being together, most of the men in uniform. Curiously, the soldiers never commented on my civilian dress, presumably just happy to be where they were with their companion.

With practice, we got better at the sex, managing to satisfy each other though intercourse nearly at the same time. Our enjoyment increased, the pleasures each was having growing more intense. Physically at least we were a happily married couple.

Dining together, we discussed my plans, especially in terms of money. Serving as a volunteer was undoubtedly public-spirited of me, but brought in no salary. The money we had brought was dwindling but Maud seemed pleased, so I guessed the money was well spent. Certainly I was happy.

Our honeymoon had gone on just over a week when I received a telegram. This was a surprise, as I didn't think anyone knew where I was, but Maud reminded me that her parents knew. Opening the telegram, I found it was from the hospital, asking me to return at once as the hospital was swamped with casualties from the latest offensive, evidently an "all hands" situation. I showed the telegram to Maud. She agreed we had to return and right away.

I apologized, but she said, "We can always come back, David. It has been very enjoyable, but if they are that desperate, then you must go."

It was late in the afternoon. We packed our things, condoms included, checked out, and boarded the first train back. We rode back in darkness. I put my arms about my wife, who napped with her head on my shoulder. Despite the recall, I was feeling very much at peace. Even with the uncertainties of the war and my official part in it, I had a partner, someone in my corner, a "yoke-mate" to paraphrase the Latin. I wasn't alone any more.

It was still dark when we reached London. Finding a taxi took some time and dawn had broken by the time we arrived at the Millens. Maud's parents were just up. They confirmed that a man from the hospital had requested our location. So, still unshaven, I picked up my medical bag, kissed my wife, and walked quickly to the hospital.

HOME SERVICE

---◆---

I was put right to work. I hadn't slept much on the train, so had been mostly awake over 24 hours. Still, the urgency of the cases kept me awake and functioning.

Patient after patient.

Opening the blankets, I had to brace myself, fearful of what I would see. Besides the wounds themselves, we were encountering many cases of the wounds becoming infected. Unless these wounds were cleaned, infection could become gangrenous and even fatal. And each case, each man, was unique.

Every hour or so, a new trainload of wounded men would arrive. Casualties had been very heavy, and from hearing some of the men talk, gains had been marginal at best. I worked on. Occasionally a nurse would bring some tea, heavily sugared to help keep me at it. At one point, I glanced out the windows and was surprised to see it was dark. I drank some more tea. I didn't bother looking at my watch. Eventually one of the senior surgeons told me to get some rest. I stretched out on a just vacated cot in a hall, fully dressed, and fell asleep. I was rousted some time later. My cot was needed for a wounded man. Again I didn't bother looking at my watch; at this point I wasn't sure what day it was. I took my medical bag, which I had used as a pillow, with me to the staff showers. I emptied my bowels and bladder, showered and shaved. My beard looked like perhaps two days' growth.

Returning to the wards, I found the situation unchanged. My reappearance was clearly welcome but otherwise unremarked. A nurse gave me some sort of bun and more tea. I realized I was very hungry but had my time fully occupied and more. I assisted with surgery after surgery. Essentially, I was now a "dresser," a surgical student. More and more, I was allowed to perform operations, routine operations, on my own: removal of shrapnel and bullets, taking great care to disinfect the wounds. With some men such a precaution was too late, so I had to reopen half-healed wounds and try to clean them before re-sewing.

I had no sense of time passing as case after case claimed my attention. I wondered if there were any of our men left. At one point I was able to obtain an actual meal, which I wolfed down before returning to the wards. I thought of sending a note to my wife but had no time. I noticed a convalescing soldier handing hard candies to other wounded men. This clearly cheered them. I thought I would try that with my patients.

It was dark outside again, so at least another day had passed. I realized I was about to collapse, so handed over to another doctor. No empty cots available, but I saw a big armchair in a staff waiting room. I sat down in that and lost consciousness. I was again awakened by one of the staff surgeons, who remarked on what he was pleased to call my laziness. I thought he was joking but couldn't be sure of that. So I stood up. The surgeon promptly took possession of the chair himself and immediately fell asleep. I went to the staff showers to recreate myself before returning to work.

Mercifully the number of wounded began to diminish. I was able to talk to another senior staff doctor about joining the Medical Service. If I was going to have to work this hard, I certainly wanted to be paid. He took his time before replying as he was indiscriminately devouring biscuits and some sandwiches, washing these down with heavily sugared tea. I was trying to do the same myself, except I was hard-pressed to get my hands on the victuals, he was so active. However, he had to stop eating to answer my question, enabling me to secure the last two sandwiches. I ate these while he said:

"Go to the War Office and tell them you want to be commissioned in the Medical Service. I will recommend you, as will Cowper and Evans, so there should be no problem."

Cowper and Evans were also senior staff doctors. They had always seemed critical of my efforts, so their endorsement was surprising.

The next day, or perhaps the day after that, I returned to the Millens. I had a shower bath first. At Maud's instance I now had baths much more often. Otherwise I badly needed clean clothing, one or preferably several nights sleep in a proper bed, actual meals and of course sex with my wife. Maud would be at work, so I went to the shop.

My father-in-law called to Maud, "David is back."

My wife promptly appeared, looked glad to see me, but said, "David, you look thin and worn. Has it been that bad?"

She put up her hand to touch my face. I kissed the hand and replied, "It was worse, worse than you could imagine. What day is it?" Maud and her father stared at me, so I explained, "I have lost all track of the time. We were on our feet day and night, eating and sleeping at odd moments, rare odd moments at that."

Maud said, "Today is Tuesday. You have been away eleven days now."

I shook my head, said, "Damn. I need clean clothes."

Maud nodded a little over emphatically, told me, "Give the dirty ones to Ma. She will have them washed for you. Aside from that, what are you going to do?"

I replied, "I will go to talk to the Royal Army Medical Corps about being commissioned. I have three recommenders, so there should be no problem. Then I will return to your parents' place. An actual meal eaten sitting down would be nice."

Maud smiled approvingly, so I went to the Millens to change my clothes.

The official I talked to about a commission indeed told me there would be no problem, given my experience and recommenders. In fact, I was able to fill out the papers then and there and was told my commission would be ready the next day. So I would have one last evening of freedom before beginning my military service.

At table, the conversation centred about my duties and my pay. Maud and I would be able to be together, even if unpredictably, if I were based in Britain. If I had to serve overseas, two weeks leave every six months would be granted. Though Maud was living with her parents, the pay would be welcome. Otherwise, the news from Maud's brother was related and discussed. So far his ships had escaped being sunk. He was still a first mate, a little young for such a senior post, so I gathered he was considered very capable.

Maude and I retired early to bed; I claimed I was worn down from the last period of working in hospital. However, in bed with my wife, I made clear I was not that debilitated. Maud was quite eager as well: she confessed she had missed me. I was pleased at this, but after, I reminded her we would be separated perhaps for months at a time. This sobered us both, but Maud remarked that millions of other couples were also separated by the war. I confessed this didn't really make me feel much better. Still, I kissed her and we fell asleep, together for the moment.

A night's sleep, together with sex with my wife, brought me to near functionality, sufficiently so I could propose we go to the jewellery store where Maud's "official" wedding ring was. We made this an outing, despite encountering comments from women who felt I should be in infantry. I had already paid for the ring and the sizing, and once I picked up the ring, I placed it on her fourth left hand finger for the second time. She would wear the plain ring on her right hand. All very romantic, and Maud permitted me to kiss her again, publicly, to the cheers of clerks and customers alike. We took our leave, arm in arm and smiling.

The next day I picked up my commission, took this to a shop to get my uniforms, badges, etc. and returned to the Millens. Mrs Millen again undertook to have the garments worn inside the uniform washed. Once these dried I would be able to look a proper soldier and could walk the streets of London without reproach.

In the meantime, a note arrived from the hospital requesting my services, so I guessed another spate of casualties had arrived. Going to the hospital, I stopped at the Millens' shop to tell Maud of the day's events and to warn her of my possible absence for an unknown period of time. I once more kissed her hand in farewell.

The situation at the hospital was as I had guessed. Heavy German counterattacks were taking their toll on our troops who were in relatively unfortified positions. I guessed the German hospitals were overwhelmed as well, but that didn't help our people. So back to work I went. The effects of the two days or so of respite vanished within a few hours, leaving me feeling as though I had never left the hospital. At least now I was being paid.

Once more I lost track of the time, patient succeeding patient. Scattered bits of food, not meals, and heavily sugared tea fuelled all our efforts, relieved by sleep or rather unconsciousness at odd times and in odd places. Then I was unexpectedly released to go back to my wife and her parents. Going out, I found it was daylight; looking at clocks, I deduced it was late afternoon.

This time Maud was less surprised when I asked her how long I had been on duty: "Six days," she said. She decided to accompany me back to her parents' place this time remarking, "I want to see you in your uniform, David. I expect you will look very dashing."

I commented. "Dash and near total exhaustion would seem irreconcilable, but I will preen and pose to my utmost."

Maud asked, "How long do you have?"

This question flummoxed me. After a minute I replied, "I really don't know. At some point, I will be given orders, posted somewhere. Right now, I am kind of a supernumerary I suppose." After some more silence, I said, "Seeing you again, I realize what my life is really all about. It is good I am worked so hard, or I would be missing you all the time."

Maud smiled and took my arm. When we reached her parents' place, we went to bed before dinner and thoroughly enjoyed each other. Then we arose for dinner, ate, and once more retired early. It wasn't a honeymoon, my job hung over both our minds but for the moment we were happy. The next day I donned my uniform, and Maud told me she thought me very handsome. I was very pleased; no one had ever characterized me thus, and I accused her of needing spectacles. To celebrate being together, we took a walk through Saint James Park, looking at the swans, the trees and the other couples. Nearly all the men were in uniform, as was I.

We were strolling, sauntering really, arm in arm, when I saw a couple approaching. The man was Landrum. I had not seen the woman before. She was well dressed. I wondered why Landrum hadn't secured a sweetheart by now. I guessed this woman wouldn't make the running either: from their demeanour, Landrum and the woman were together physically yet not together emotionally. Maud noticed them also. And Landrum saw us. He headed toward us, the woman following. Maud had let go of my arm and put her right hand over her left as though to conceal her wedding ring, the one that had to be shrunk to fit her finger. Maud and Landrum had locked gazes. I was becoming upset. He looked dashing and of course handsome; he had been decorated, I saw. He was close to us now. He and my wife seemed fixed on each other, as though there was no one else in the world.

I was about to step between them when the woman accompanying Landrum spoke: "Peter." At this, Landrum turned to the woman and introduced us to her and her to us, again referring to me as an old schoolmate. I told them that Maud was now my wife. I could not interpret Maud's and Landrum's expressions when I said this. Then they moved off, Landrum and my wife still looking at each other. We finally continued on our walk, though for me the day, perhaps the week, was ruined. I was hurt. I was angry. An old wound had been reopened. Maud did not take my arm again as we walked in silence back through the streets.

At length she spoke, "There is a chips shop ahead. I am hungry."

I was silent, finally speaking, "As you wish."

Maud looked at me, seemed about to make light of my feelings, thought better of it and took my arm as we entered the chips shop. The food was served cafeteria-style, on trays. I was actually hungry myself, though my feelings of jealousy damped the hunger. We ate in sullen silence. I really didn't know what to say. Maud knew my feelings about Landrum; it would be pointless to upbraid her again. And, depending on where I was posted, this might be the last time we were together for a while. And I did love her. What was the expression, "love slavery"? I was beginning to understand what that meant. Finally, I realized that if my wife couldn't be trusted to remain faithful, there was nothing for it but divorce. And heartbreak.

On the way back, Maud was sensitive enough of my feelings to take my arm once more. I strove for a lighter mood, without much success. I stayed silent until I could talk to her without quarrelling. At her parents' home I found a letter awaiting me from the Medical Corps. I opened and read it. I had hoped to serve at a hospital in England, preferably London, but knew the chances were that I would be assigned to a hospital in France. This proved to be the case. I would have to leave by tomorrow evening. I handed the letter to Maud and stood in silence while she read it.

At length she handed the letter back saying, "At least you won't be in the fighting."

I couldn't tell from her tone how she felt about this. Was she glad for me or contemptuous of me? Finally I was able to speak seriously but civilly: "Dear, we have little time together left. From what I hear, my duties will expose me to some risk and will keep me away for months. What would you like to do? A film, a play, a concert? We can dine wherever you wish."

Maud smiled, the atmosphere in the room brightened, and she replied, "I will have to see to your things. Then we can eat here and perhaps retire early."

I smiled too, bent to kiss her, did so, the kiss became an invitation and we went up to her bedroom. My things would have to wait.

We stood facing each other at the train station. It was an emotional moment for us both. I asked her, "Write to me often. I will write to you when my duties permit. At times, I will hardly have time to sit down, from what I have experienced. At other times I will be utterly bored. At all times I will miss you."

I thought there were traces of tears in her eyes, we embraced and kissed and I boarded my train with the other soldiers. I didn't see Landrum. I wasn't sure whether I was glad of this or the reverse.

OVERSEAS SERVICE

I dozed on the train ride, on the boat ride, then again on the train in France. We often sat on sidings, and when we did move, it was slowly. When I wasn't napping, I stared out the windows at the French countryside, soldiers and their gear everywhere. It was a relief to get off the train. I began inquiring about the location of the hospital to which I had been assigned. Eventually, I collected enough information to set out for the place. I rode in motor lorries and was finally able to walk to the place, carrying my things.

The hospital, a collection of obviously hastily constructed buildings and some tents, was busy. At length I located the man in charge, waited until he had finished with a soldier whose chest had been opened by shrapnel, apparently a successful operation, and reported myself. He seemed irritable, told me, "You should have been here yesterday evening, Mendy."

I flushed, replied, "I arrived here as fast as the trains allowed, Sir."

He was clearly angered at my apparent presumption, but accepted a mug of hot tea from a nurse, drank it, drank some more, then said in a more amicable tone, "They are slow at times. Very well, since you are here, I want you to go right away to one of the Advanced Dressing Stations and stay until relieved. My second will show you where to go."

I nodded, said, "Yes, Sir," and went to find his deputy.

I was surprised to find this was a woman, a senior nurse. I told her, "I am Doctor David Mendy, reporting for duty. I was told to go to one of the Advanced Dressing Stations and stay until relieved."

The woman nodded and said, "I will send you with an orderly as guide. The doctor who was there was wounded." This was unwelcome news but I only nodded.

The orderly in question was eating a sandwich and almost simultaneously drinking what appeared to be tea. He gestured for me to follow him. I deposited my bag and took my medical gear. I also managed to secure two sandwiches and a mug of tea and ate and drank as we set out. The sandwiches were ham and the tea was heavily sugared, which made me feel much more active.

We advanced into the darkness. Flashes from guns, explosions of shells gave some idea of what we were walking over. We were going overland, my guide explained, as the communication trenches were regularly shelled, especially at night, when movements of men occurred. Even so, there was plenty of shell craters scattered, apparently at random, everywhere else.

The Advanced Dressing Station was perhaps 400 yards behind the front line. It had a floor that was two or so feet below ground, walls built of sandbags, very thick walls, the roof of many heavy beams reinforced with pit props, covered with a thick layer of more sandbags. My guide said, "Both sides refrain from deliberately shelling medical facilities, but sometimes shells fall short or long. So this is built to resist a near miss."

I asked, "What about a direct hit?"

The orderly smiled grimly and replied, "It won't withstand that."

Inside were many cots, most with wounded men on them. There were blankets on the floor for overflows. Some men were groaning but most were stoical, enduring their injuries. The place stank: urine, faeces, blood, vomit, and disinfectant, with a leaden base of the smells of unwashed men. In a corner was a stove, several pots steaming on it.

I was greeted with relief by two orderlies already there. They directed me to the most serious cases. Some of these men were by now beyond help: large doses of morphine were all I could provide. I went from man to man, cleaning and bandaging wounds, occasionally sedating men to remove bullets or shrapnel where I thought prompt action necessary.

Every so often, stretcher bearers would bring another man in. Wounded men were supposed to be given preliminary care at regimental aid posts, but I saw no evidence of this. So the men brought to us had to be treated right away. And as free stretcher bearers appeared, I would send wounded men back to where ambulances waited. I had pots of water boiling, using the boiled water, once it had cooled enough, to clean around the wounds to try to forestall gangrene. The men's skins were filthy and I soon discovered the men were lousy: I could see the lice and the nits and the eggs.

One of the pots was used to make tea, which I gave to every man who was conscious and not suffering from stomach wounds. This was sugared to near the consistency of treacle. I wasn't sure of the medical value of this concoction, but it was well received. There wasn't enough space on the stove for more than tea, no Bovril or Oxo.

The two orderlies who had been there originally were clearly near collapse, so I told them to sleep on the blankets on the floor. I and the orderly who had guided me worked on and on, each case its own world. At some point, stretcher bearers brought in a man through the blankets that served as a door and I realized it was day.

Gradually things became less chaotic. Dead soldiers were taken outside for burial, the worst cases were taken on to the ambulances then to the Casualty Clearing Station once I thought they could be moved, and everyone else was sleeping or drinking tea. I began to imagine things were coming under control. Not before time, as I was becoming exhausted as was my orderly.

I had the two original orderlies rousted, and lay down myself on a blanket on the floor. The blanket stank but by now I didn't care. Almost immediately, it seemed, I was rousted myself: three more wounded men, one near death from haemorrhage. I worked demonically to save him and to treat the others. More stretcher bearers were recruited to move the less seriously wounded men once darkness fell. I was told by the stretcher bearers that the communication trenches were too narrow: men moving up the line and stretcher bearers moving in the opposite direction were constantly in each other's way. This wore the stretcher bearers out faster but there wasn't anything I could do about the situation. And this was considered a quiet sector!

We were beginning to run short of medical supplies, tea and sugar. I wrote out a list, surprised at how shaky my handwriting was, asking that these items be sent by the returning ambulances and stretcher bearers. I tried to clean up the place, having bed bottles emptied, faeces collected with a shovel, the filthiest blankets taken outside at least for airing. If it rained, maybe they would be washed somewhat, though drying them after would be very difficult.

There was a desk and chair in the place where I could sit and write my requests. When things slowed sufficiently, I crossed my arms on the desk top, lay my head down on my crossed arms and slept until the next casualty arrived or emergency occurred, or until I was awakened by nightmares.

Otherwise, I was feeling relieved to some extent: I had been able to deal with the situation, I hoped effectively. Treating freshly wounded men hadn't been much worse than I had experienced at Charing Cross. I had worried about how I would handle the responsibility of working on my own, but I hadn't been paralyzed by shock or indecision. My training at Charing Cross had been adequate, at least for a relative trickle of casualties.

I was able to rotate the orderlies, ensuring that the two up had been rested. I myself was feeling less ready to collapse. Replacement supplies were coming in and were stored in a more systematic fashion. We were beginning to build up our reserves. I was able to give each new casualty more thorough treatment, particularly in cleaning the wounds and the skin around them. Though I was not a surgeon, I was able to remove some pieces of shrapnel and bullets.

A medical officer carrying a medical bag appeared. He looked around, seemed offended by the smells, and then advanced to me. "I am here to relieve you," he said.

I got up from the desk, feeling very stiff. We had a dozen men awaiting removal to the Casualty Clearing Station. I described each man's condition, showed my replacement where our supplies were, introduced him to the two orderlies who were to remain and left with the third.

Outside, it was dark again, though I had once more lost track of how many days I had been there. Despite the danger, we went back using the communication trench. Groups of men moving in the opposite direction were encountered often, but didn't slow us much. I badly needed a bath, my clothes needed boiling, I could feel the lice moving over my skin, an awful sensation, and I wanted decent meals and a real bed, or at least a cot. The occasional shells exploding nearby I ignored. I was now an experienced front-line soldier, I felt.

I couldn't get a ride in an ambulance so had to walk the entire ten miles or so. I was tired when I began this trek and exhausted when I reached the hospital. The chief was apparently abed, sensible man. His deputy told me I had been at the Advanced Dressing Station seventeen days, which caused me to shake my head in amazement. She also told me where my room was, that my bag was there and that I had some mail. I said, "I badly need a bath, something to eat and about a month's sleep."

She smiled and told me I had done very well and that future rotations would last no more than a week.

I remarked, "When business is brisk, even two or three days seem endless."

A nurse carrying a large teapot and a tray of mugs offered each of us some tea. The deputy and I both accepted; I drank three mugful's almost without pausing as I discovered I was thirsty as Hell. The sugar in the tea helped revive me and I left for my quarters.

Clean clothes, a hot shower bath and a shave did even more toward restoring me. My filthy clothes would be boiled. The mail consisted of a letter from my half-sister and another from Maud, most welcome. My half-sister wrote in careful cursive, telling me how proud she was of me, which cheered me and made me smile. My wife's letter was on the short side, but then not much had happened in the 2 ½ weeks since we had parted:

10 February, 1916

Dear David

My brother appeared a few days ago. His ship was stopped by a German U-boat and the crew ordered to lifeboats before the U-boat sank the ship. My brother said the Germans were very correct and even considerate, making sure the crew had water and food and blankets. Even so, my brother and the rest of the crew drifted two days before rescue. Now he is waiting for a new ship.

Mother and I have begun keeping the books for other shops for extra money. I am not criticising you in doing this, your allowance is generous; it is just that I would have nothing to do for much of the day. And seeing how other shops are managed is sometimes useful.

Please write and tell me what you are doing and where you are. The newspapers say not much is happening. Have you been able to eat at any French restaurants? Is their cooking so very much better than English cooking?

Maud

I shook my head; I would have a great deal to tell her, if I could remember it. Two buns and more tea however seemed to make me drowsy and I decided to reply tomorrow. I went to my

room, again sort of a courtesy room, sat down on the cot then lay
down and was awakened several times by nightmares. I realized
this must mean I was sleeping.

The next morning I secured some breakfast and wrote a reply
to Rose and to my wife. I figured I had better write now before
reporting to the chief doctor as he would undoubtedly put me
right to an endless succession of tasks. The letter to Rose praised
the clarity of her handwriting and thanked her for her praise.
I added that her praise was likely all I would get, so was very
welcome.

I had more to say to my wife:

14 February, 1916

Dear Maud

*Business at my shop was very brisk indeed, of the
lose-track-of-time intensity. Meals? I must have eaten
something sometime, as I am still alive. Sleep? There must
have been some, but the 17 days I was on continuous duty
is mercifully a blur. So no, I wasn't able to compare French
cuisine to ours. I am now back at hospital to be given new
tasks.*

*If you are going to be going into the bookkeeping
business, you should consider taking courses in
bookkeeping, if only for the formal credentials, as these
would attract more business. I was a little surprised at
your decision as I thought the books at your father's shop
kept you busy.*

*Pray give my regards to your parents and to your
brother. My love is of course yours.*

David

I could have written a great deal more, but I guessed the chief
wanted me to report without obvious delay. So I posted my letters
and went in search of him. As I expected, he was surveying the
wards; also as I expected, he seemed short tempered, so I waited

until he drank his morning mug of tea before appearing before him.

"Ah, Mendy. Sorry we left you so long but we were badly short-handed. You seem to have handled the situation well, from what I hear, so all's well and all that. Take charge of the Third Ward and assist in the surgery. We will send you back to one of the Advanced Dressing Stations when the schedule is worked out. That is all."

I said, "Thank you, Sir," and went to find the Third Ward.

I circulated, talking to all the men who were awake, looking at everyone's wounds, reading their charts. Most would be shipped home as soon as they could be transported safely. A few needed more surgery, removal of deeply buried shrapnel or in a few cases amputations. I was glad that none of the men I had been responsible for had developed infected wounds.

Many of the men who were awake were exchanging experiences with each other. Everyone seemed good humoured, aware they were lucky to be sent home with "blighty" wounds. All were looking forward to seeing home, friends, family, and sweethearts again. Listening to some of them, I heard accents I recognized: these were men from the two hostile parishes I had grown up in, talking amicably, laughing and chaffing the nurses. I recognized some of these men in fact and they recognized me. We exchanged smiles, greetings, and handshakes. The feud between the two parishes was clearly over as far as these men were concerned. So the war had done something toward breaking down tribal feelings, which I thought was good.

Casualties were brought in, an erratic trickle: men in the wrong place when a shell burst. Sniper casualties usually died, so we didn't see many of those. This was as well, as head injuries could be hard to treat. I helped the surgeons as much as possible, to improve my skills when I went back to the Advanced Dressing Station. Until then I was almost on holiday: light duties, regular meals, and reasonable opportunities for sleep. Occasionally I would be assigned night duty, but not often.

It couldn't last; the chief's deputy told me one afternoon I was to return to the Advanced Dressing Station that night. So I packed my things, much better informed as to what I would need. Then I finished my letter to my wife and posted it. I ate my last decent meal for a while, dozed on my cot until full dark and set out. I was alone this time.

I managed to obtain a ride most of the way on a motor ambulance. I got out and walked along the communication trench to the ADS. I dodged stretchers, frequently passed groups of soldiers trudging up the line burdened with rifle and pack. Flashes from guns and exploding shells gave barely enough light. Desultory shelling, I thought.

On two occasions shells burst close enough to cause us to duck. This was involuntary; if my luck was out, I would be dead before I could react. When I arrived at the Station I was greeted with joy by the doctor on duty, not the one who had relieved me. There were only five or six casualties awaiting removal to the Casualty Clearing Station. The doctor went over each case; everything seemed under control, but that was a fragile situation. One unlucky hit and I and the two orderlies left with me would be overwhelmed.

I set up pots of water to boil, surprised that the doctor I had relieved hadn't left any. I arranged my instruments, set my bag on a cot to serve as a pillow, and then talked to the two orderlies. They seemed rested. I prepared a large pot of tea and opened a bag of sugar, poured it into a tin, and then sealed it. This was because the steam from the pots of water would turn exposed sugar to syrup. Then after checking each of the waiting wounded, I appointed one orderly to be on duty. I and the other would nap.

Twice I was awakened by incoming casualties, more "blighty" wounds. I was careful to wash around the wounds with the boiled water then the Dakin's solution, this after washing my hands first. Stretcher bearers took all our wounded away, leaving our station empty for the first time in my experience. By now it was dawn and the three of us turned to cleaning up the station, including washing the blankets and the cots themselves. The place certainly smelled better.

Over the course of the day we had more business including a man with his belly sliced open so the intestines were piled on him when he was brought in. This looked awful, but I washed them, reinserted them and sewed the man up. He was still alive after all this, so I sent him back feeling somewhat hopeful. Two men had badly shattered arms. I feared the arms would be amputated but did my best to put them back together, finally splinting the arms after sewing up the wounds. The remaining cases weren't so demanding, but by the end of the day I was beginning to recognize the beginnings of exhaustion. However I had to continue, napping when I could.

Day by day, night by night, quiet periods were randomly punctuated by busy ones, occasionally frantic ones. The two orderlies were relieved; stretcher bearers came and went with their burdens. On two occasions shells exploded near enough to jolt the ground. I lived on biscuits and heavily sugared tea. No change of clothing, and I could start to feel the lice. So when my relief arrived, I was quite ready to return to the hospital.

For some reason the German guns were much more active as I went back. The shells seemed to fall much closer to the communication trench. There would be a flash, a jolt closely followed by a roar, spurts of dirt and shrapnel. I began to try to be as small as possible. Still the same traffic along the trench, no sign of any casualties yet but that couldn't last. There was no point in stopping. I guessed the odds of being hit by shrapnel were the same moving or stationary unless I lay down and hid in a shell crater. Since these all had water in them, this was not inviting.

I came to where ambulances were waiting. I was able to ride most of the way back in an ambulance, horse-drawn this time. It seemed a very long journey. I gradually realized we were out of easy range of the German guns and began to feel less afraid. Dawn was on the horizon when I reached the hospital. I obtained a most welcome, early breakfast, and then bathed and dressed in clean, lice-free clothes. Life could begin again.

I had time to write to Maud and to my father, step-mother and half-sister. In fact, despite aggressive circulation though the wards, I had time for naps, indeed time for boredom. I discussed with some colleagues a proposal to go to the nearest large French town, Amiens, to dine, but we couldn't do that right away as emergencies kept arising. This was unfortunate as the meals there, I was assured, were first rate.

My next letter from Maud described her and her mother's new clients, nearby shops, and her routine. The extra work was not so much for the money as to stay busy. She worried about her brother, once again at sea. I noticed she was not worried about me, which was a bit humiliating. I thought of enlightening her about the real dangers I was facing but decided I didn't want to add to her worries. She said she would indeed take a bookkeeping course that was offered. She ended her letter saying she missed me, yet I thought her statement somewhat perfunctory. Or was I again imagining things?

We rotated duties at the hospital, the Casualty Clearing Stations and the Advanced Dressing Stations. One week at each was the routine, still light casualties overall, although rumours were strengthening about a big offensive in the works in our sector. I remembered my first period of duty in the Advanced Dressing Station and became apprehensive. What was planned would produce a situation that was vastly worse. However, sufficient to the day . . . Like the soldiers, I had become fatalistic, taking advantage of any easing of my duties.

Days passed, weeks passed, months came and went. I was definitely becoming more proficient at treating the casualties. I felt I was an accepted part of the staff. At the same time, the rumours of the projected offensive gained in detail and were backed up by obvious preparations, proliferation of artillery and greatly increased numbers of infantry. The talk was of late spring for the start of the offensive, so hopefully I would be able to secure some leave before it began. I knew the crush of casualties would be overwhelming, no matter how successful we were and I wanted to be well rested.

The exchange of letters with my wife continued. I detected a warmer tone in her letters. She again said she missed me and asked when I would get leave. I replied that I was doing my best not to think of her at every spare moment and that when my leave would occur was entirely out-with my control. I asked her to think about where she wanted to go and what she wanted to do aside from the obvious which I was also trying very hard not to think about.

FIRST LEAVE

———◆———

I had been in service more than six months when I was suddenly told my leave started at that moment. I had actually prepared for the event, with a packed suitcase waiting by my cot. So I picked it up and caught a ride in a lorry; I was going home at last, even if for only two weeks.

Though the systems for rotation had been in operation long enough to be fairly efficient, my journey still seemed interminable. I was quite impatient by the time we pulled into the station in London. It was near noon and I booked a taxi despite the expense. I hauled my suitcase out, overpaid the driver and walked into the Millens' shop. Mr Millen saw me, hailed me, extended his hand, shook it and called his daughter: "Maud! David's here."

There was a curtain separating the office where Maud worked from the rest of the store. This was switched aside by a slender arm and there she was. I thought my jaw would drop off my face, I was grinning so hard. Her face had lit up and I bent over the counter to kiss her. Her mouth was slightly opened in invitation, not that such was necessary.

"God, I've missed you," I said and she smiled.

Half an hour later we lay in each other's arms, sweaty and relaxed.

I said, "I hope I haven't disrupted the path of commerce too much."

My wife said, "Not really. What I don't do today I will tomorrow. End of the month is the busy time. How long do you have?"

I replied, "Two weeks. Have you thought of things to do?"

Maud said, "At the moment, what we just did is all I want to do."

I was very pleased indeed. We kissed and slept until dinner.

At table, Mrs Millen told me that Maud's brother would be home as well in two days. He was still a first mate but getting work. No suggestion of a sweetheart as yet, but if he were at sea much of the time, that was not surprising. Mrs Millen asked me if there was any danger in what I did. I was very happy to answer her:

"About one week in three, I work at what we call an Advanced Dressing Station, where we basically keep wounded men alive until we can get them to a proper hospital. That is fairly close to the front line, well within artillery range."

I took a drink and continued, "Of course no one deliberately targets medical facilities, but sometimes shells are misaimed. On a few occasions, shells have landed close enough to shake the place."

I felt Maud's gaze on me, clearly she was impressed.

I went on, "Coming and going from the Dressing Stations, I and everyone else use communication trenches at night. The Germans of course know men are moving along these, so regularly shell them. Since it is dark, their fire tends to be inaccurate, because they can't see to correct their aim. So everyone tends to push on irrespective of the shelling, figuring that if the shell lands close enough, our time is done, we can't take cover fast enough. Occasionally a shell will land in a communication trench, causing injuries or deaths, but that is just a risk everyone assumes."

I looked at my wife and smiled. She reached over and squeezed my hand. Our eyes met and I saw respect there.

She asked, "David, have you ever seen the front line?"

I was slightly deflated, shook my head and replied, "No. My orders require me to be at the Dressing Station all the time, because that is where wounded men are brought and I must be available. From what I have heard, serving at the front line or in the support or reserve lines is boring and exhausting. Conditions are filthy: within a few days, lice become a major nuisance. That is why troops are rotated often, so men are on front line duty no more than a week. They spend another week in support and two in reserve, where they can bathe and boil their clothing."

Maud and her parents were silent. Maud then said, "But there are facilities for bathing at the Dressing Station, aren't there?"

I answered, "No. The Dressing Stations are basically in holes in the ground, roofs very heavily enforced with pit props and covered with a thick layer of sandbags. That is just to protect against near misses: a direct hit with a large calibre shell would probably kill everyone inside."

I drank some more milk then continued, "The men at the front and in support also live in thickly covered holes in the ground. Sanitation, still less comfort, is a distant second to safety."

The others at the table were silent, digesting this.

I said, "So you see that even with my relatively diluted experience of life at the front, I am very, very glad to be home, here, even if for only a few days."

Maud and I again exchanged smiles. She now had a much more accurate idea of how we all lived and I could see the respect she had gained for me was still there. I felt reassured. I wasn't just a sort of military servant, but to some extent was regarded as a soldier too.

The next day, Maud basically declared holiday so we could be together. We took walks, dined at whatever restaurant rumour hinted served at least passable food, attended concerts and one or two plays. I didn't see Landrum; presumably he was serving. I had no idea when his leaves would occur and didn't want to know.

Maud's brother appeared. Maud and I were usually out, so our contact with him was at meals, where his mother asked him about his experiences. Essentially they were the same as mine, hours of often boring work punctuated by occasional terrifying ones. Underlying was the realization that we were all subject to chance, to odds; we were merely pieces on some cosmological gaming board. I made this comment to my wife one night after we had enjoyed each other.

She was silent, and then asked, "Then what does it all mean? What is our purpose after all? Do you believe in God?"

I was silent in turn before replying, "I was never one to think about such things, just to accept Christian doctrine. I suppose I can only say I have duties, to our country, to my patients, to you, and can only push blindly on, trying to fulfil these. Not very profound, I admit, but all I can find to justify my work and my life."

More silence until I said, "Dear, I apologize for the philosophical gloom. We are together again, in each other's arms and, dammit, love must matter too."

I could feel my wife smile and held her more closely.

We spent the rapidly passing days as before: taking walks, dining at any restaurant that looked interesting, attending concerts and a play, one of Shaw's. As I expected, this prompted conversation: my wife was, I once more noted, an intelligent, reflective woman. She seemed to enjoy our promenades, since I was in uniform, and she even commented she was proud and happy to be seen with me. This made me proud and happy to have so pretty a wife.

On occasion, she did have some work to do, at her families' shop or at one or another shop she did the books for. During one of these episodes, I went to the jewellery store where I had gotten the proposal broach, for that is what its purchase had led to, and bought another jewelled pin, this time a bee. I put a note in the box, saying it reminded me of her, busy and beautiful.

This was very well received as I had hoped, but I had basically wanted to please her, to make her happy. She assured me I had been successful, as we stood on the platform next to my train. We embraced and kissed as though it might be the last time, and there was some chance that would be the case. I watched her as long as possible, and then sat heavily down on my seat. Everyone else in my compartment was sombre as well; God only knew when or if we would be reunited with our loved ones.

ONCE MORE . . .

Back in France, I resumed my duties. Tensions were much greater, partly because there wasn't much business yet to keep us occupied. Wounded were shipped out as soon as possible, to keep bed space clear. I was able to assist in several surgeries and was struck by the increase in skill of our surgeons: practice definitely helped.

Rotations went on as before. I suggested to the chief doctor that adding a second or even a third doctor to the Advanced Dressing Stations once the offensive began would be very helpful; though everyone seemed confident our casualties would be light. Our preparations were indeed impressive, thousands of guns, tens of millions of shells and hundreds of thousands of men.

The men were the most impressive: big, strong, high spirited and well equipped. The higher ranking generals were cheered: clearly morale was very high. Everyone was eager to strike, to attack the German lines. I mentioned all this in the letters to Maud, though cautioning her not to chatter about what I said to others. Not that my admonitions were really necessary: my wife was not a chatterbox.

Our offensive began with an enormous artillery barrage.
The sky to our rear was bright as day with gun flashes, and in
the Dressing Station we could not make ourselves heard without
shouting because of the noise. The stretcher bearers, messengers
and others passing through thought no Germans would be left to
oppose our advance.

The barrage went on and on, day following night following
day. We were told the advance would begin at 7:30 in the morning,
1 July. The attack had been postponed two days for some reason.
Indeed, our fire even increased, hard for us to believe after the last
week. I, the other two doctors and the attendants in our Station
waited nervously. I was in charge. I thought all our preparations
were made, all cots empty, every pot filled with boiling water,
instruments sterilized and covered, several gallons of tea made. I
had the tea made double strength in tea with about six times the
sugar.

We knew there would be a rush of custom, but we were
not prepared for the numbers: hundreds of men, some walking
wounded, some on stretchers, some carried over other men's
shoulders, some in carts or barrows. One man, with a shattered
leg, had crawled the entire distance. The walking wounded were
bandaged by our attendants. We gave these some tea and sent them
on their way. The more serious cases, nearly all bullet wounds,
we worked on to get fit to be transported back to the Casualty
Clearing Station.

Our cots filled almost immediately, and then we had to set
men on stretchers on the floor, or on a ground sheet laid directly
on the floor as we began to run short of stretchers.

In fact, we heard over and over from the stretcher bearers that
with reinforcements trying to get to the line, the communication
trenches were too narrow to permit movement both ways. We
heard this with mixed emotions: men were going to die because
they couldn't be brought to us fast enough, but we were better able
to deal with the men who made it to us.

I had laid in more than ample stocks of bandages, lint, Dakin's
solution, everything we would need, or so I had imagined, yet our

supplies shrank very rapidly. I began snatching spare moments to write notes requesting more supplies, sending these with the stretcher bearers taking men on to hospital and asking the bearers to bring the supplies back. I prayed the hospital's supplies weren't becoming exhausted as well.

We worked on and on and on, each new case its own emergency, no idea of the time, taking a few minutes' sleep in shifts, sitting at the table with our head cradled on our arms. I became aware that the tea we had prepared was greatly favoured, very cheering to the wounded that could drink and most refreshing to the rest of us. My notes now were requesting tea and sugar as well, underlined though the stretcher bearers were aware of their importance.

We had again run out of Dakin's solution, so had to use water that had been boiled and sufficiently (barely) cooled. So my messages via stretcher bearers once more included Dakin's and of course water in any form is heavy. Otherwise, our water came from a well at a nearby wrecked farmhouse. More work for orderlies and stretcher bearers.

A padre came in, took a mugful of our tea, then began assisting us, bringing tea to the wounded, talking to them, in one or two cases administering Last Rites, I hoped unnecessarily. At some point we were standing together, each with a fresh mugful, and he began to talk to me about what he had seen at the front.

I noticed his hand was shaking as he said, "Our attack in the sector I was in failed completely. Not an inch of ground gained. I went over under a flag of truce to comfort our wounded. Some other men, stretcher bearers, were bringing a few men back. Not a shot from the Germans. Our men, hundreds of them, lay in rows. I saw that many of them had fallen, then pulled ground sheets out and rolled onto these. The men all had opened Bibles in their hands. I believe they were reading these as they died. They knew their last hour had come."

I could see he was shaken by what he had seen. I was shaken myself, imagining what those men felt, the pain of their wounds, knowing that their attack had failed, seeking comfort from the

Scriptures as the blackness enveloped them. I knew the mental image his words had created in my mind would persist, perhaps over my entire life. Then more cases arrived. Men, their eyes death-shadowed, who had somehow endured hours (days?) lying on the battlefield.

Some new arrivals: men on their feet, apparently unhurt. What were they doing here? Then I recognized one of them: a fellow doctor. We were being relieved. I could not remember how long we had been on duty, not that it mattered. I took the new men around, describing each of our cases, then gathered my gear and went out with my colleagues. It was dark except for the flashes from cannon fire, ours and the Germans, shell bursts here and there. It was almost pretty at least at a distance.

At the Casualty Clearing Station, we were told to go to the big hospital near Amiens and assist there. The hospital was overwhelmed by the casualties as well. We climbed into a lorry taking men to Amiens, some perhaps wounded though everyone seemed happy to be going that way. I and the colleagues who had been assisting me slumped onto each other and slept.

At the hospital we were able to bathe and shave and don clean clothes before being set to work again. Despite the sleep we had gotten, none of us felt rested. We dragged on through the day, stopping only for brief meals. I could not remember having anything to eat at the Advanced Dressing Station once our attack had begun, so we should have been quite hungry.

Despite the crush of casualties, we slowly recovered. The numbers seemed less though still high; was this because our attacks were more successful or simply because our numbers had fallen so much? The men seemed fractionally more optimistic: we were advancing though very slowly and at heavy cost in casualties.

A letter from my wife reached me. She said she imagined I was too busy to write, she quite understood, but she would appreciate just a line to tell her I was well. I was pleased and touched by the tone of the letter. Clearly she missed me. Well, I missed her too and managed to fill a page, telling her the results of our first day's attack were beyond nightmarish, we had worked perhaps without sleep for days until relieved, and I was now basically following some of the same men I had treated earlier. I ended by saying, "I try not to think of you, because I miss you so much it is almost unbearable. Unfortunately my attempts to put you from my mind fail, and often."

Back at the Advanced Dressing Station, still in the same place though our line had advanced a mile or so. The bearers had to carry our wounded farther, over very badly cratered ground. Happily there were fewer wounded (there could hardly have been more), and our double-strength tea was very helpful in reviving everyone. Our replacements had made it up with much less sugar and the prescribed strength of tea. They were surprised by the complaints.

Our attacks persisted. New men were sent out after the usual hopefully crushing barrage only to discover the Germans were very strongly and deeply entrenched. Still we edged forward, to the point where we would need to move our Station. For that we needed work troops, engineers. We were relieved again before the new Station was complete. This time we went to the Casualty Clearing Station.

My efforts at the Advanced Dressing Station received some praise. My attention to cleaning the wounds and around them had been noticed. Men I had treated were much less likely to have wounds turn septic. I was even asked to describe what I did to the other doctors. I was pleased by this, being vain, and told Maud about my bit of recognition.

Her next letter said she was proud of my efforts. She went on to tell me of her and her mother's bookkeeping ventures. They were becoming better known and were getting more work. She named some of the shops, all unfamiliar to me. It occurred to me to ask if I should be sending her more money. I had been thinking she didn't need much, living at home, but perhaps I was taking things for granted.

The new Advanced Dressing Station was very like the old: same smells, same sounds, same sights, and the same heavy, steamy atmosphere from the pots of boiling water. I had more pots put on and with my colleagues set to dealing with the wounded. Since we were fresh, we were able to get ahead of the numbers and even cleared a few cots. We used these ourselves to sleep on, in shifts. So this rotation wasn't so bad. However we heard of yet another attack being planned for our sector and hoped we wouldn't have to deal directly with the consequences. We went back to the Casualty Clearing Station much happier.

To our relief, the new offensive began almost immediately once we returned to the Casualty Clearing Station. It had been mostly cleared in anticipation, and filled up again almost immediately. The same story: minor gains at very heavy cost. I think we all began to sense that offensives needed to be carried out differently, though we weren't clear as to exactly how.

No letter from Maud, and I was worked off my feet dealing with the men brought in. Then I was ordered back to the Advanced Dressing Station as our colleagues who had relieved us were on or past the point of collapse. So I packed extra tea and sugar and a few other luxuries such as hard candies that I knew would hearten the men, and set out with my crew.

It looked a very busy night and our progress was slow with all the traffic in the opposite direction. It was near dawn when we arrived, and the men we were relieving were furious, since they would have to spend another day here. I told them the truth, that we had come as fast as conditions permitted, without effect. One of them threatened to bring me under charges. I became angry at this and told the fellow to do as he wished but to get out of our way as we had work to do. I had an impression of near-hysteria and was not surprised to see evidence of slackness everywhere. So I and my crew set to putting things to rights, in addition to dealing with constant acute medical issues. I was very glad when the men we were replacing left the next evening.

We had been on duty perhaps four days when one of the returning stretcher bearers handed me a note. Most unwelcome news: we would have to stay here more than two weeks, there were too few replacements. I showed the note to the others at spare moments. I heard some curses that were new to me, but that was the only benefit.

We kept things moving somehow. I was actually beginning to feel my crew was an exceptionally good one, everyone knew his job, no wasted time, absolute almost uncanny cooperation. Naps were all we had but these were just across the edge of being sufficient.

The men to relieve us also appeared near dawn, but instead of a temper tantrum, I welcomed the opportunity to integrate them into our ways of doing things. I didn't know any of them but some appeared experienced and the number of casualties seemed to be dropping. So we left the next evening, full dark, walking back along the communication trench as fast as we could manage.

12

BLIGHTY WOUND

German shelling seemed heavier than usual, but we pressed on. In addition, they were firing shrapnel, which was a little more worrisome, possibly countering the protection given by the communication trench. However, as I had told Maud, it was all chance. We were up to the ruins of a brick building to my right when there was a flash against the brick wall, a concussive roar, and I was hit hard in my right shoulder. This knocked me sideways. I knew right away I had been hit by a piece of shrapnel. I hoped I wouldn't lose the arm even as the pain began. I was still on my feet so kept walking even as I began to feel blood flowing down the arm.

I tried to move my arm, succeeded in swinging it in front of me so decided to continue. If I lay down, the wound would get dirty. I would probably be stepped on, and God only knew how long it would take for someone to notice me and take me to an ambulance. The pain kept increasing. Each slight jolt (like from setting one foot down after another), set off nerves. I had been carrying my things in a bag in my right hand, so I shifted it to my left hand and inserted my right hand into my belt to ease the pull on my shoulder. I felt these did help.

It seemed a very long walk even without having to step aside for groups of men moving up the line, stepping around stretcher bearers that were resting their backs and arms before proceeding. I hoped and prayed I could make it without fainting or collapsing. I couldn't see my colleagues, we had gotten separated, so no help there.

I was beginning to stagger, to the point of attracting the attention of some stretcher bearers returning to the front. I said, "I took some shrapnel in my right shoulder. I'm going to need to be carried to an ambulance."

They looked at each other, then set their stretcher down on the ground and with professional gentleness helped me lie down on the stretcher, my bag on my stomach, and lifted me. At this point I must have fainted.

When I was conscious again, I was on a ship; I could feel it pitching and rolling. I hoped I wouldn't become sick. Looking to my right, I could see my shoulder wound had been dressed. To my great relief, I could move my right hand, so everything was still attached. I stayed awake as the ship docked and my stretcher among many others was moved onto a train. My shoulder hurt even more, keeping me from dozing, so I watched England pass the train window. I was removed from the train in London, transferred to a modified lorry, taken to Charing Cross, which of course I knew well, then moved to a cot. I lay, staring at the activity, also familiar, though from a different perspective. I wondered how soon Maud would be told where I was and why.

It was late afternoon when I arrived, early evening before an overly busy surgeon looked at my wound. He nodded, told the nurse to bandage me again and give me some morphine, a light dose, once I had eaten. This was done and I lay relaxed, drifting, drifting—almost comfortable.

Morning, the morphine had worn off. I had again managed to eat, very awkward without full use of my right arm, and then lay sweating and hurting. I had also managed to use the bed bottle;

soon I would need a bed pan. Then Maud appeared and I smiled at her. I couldn't help that. She looked upset. She was wearing a dress I had not seen before, colour and trim reminiscent of something, I couldn't remember what, and the daisy pin was on awry.

I took her hand in my left, kissed her hand. She smiled briefly and bent down and kissed me, also briefly. I commented, "That dress looks expensive." It appeared to be silk, grey with blue trim.

She looked confused, said, "Some of the shops I work in want better dress on the people working there."

This seemed a bit odd but I observed, "Your pin is on crooked."

She looked down, removed it and reattached it correctly, and then told me, "I just received the telegram from the War Office saying you were wounded and in hospital, I guessed it was this one. I suppose I was flustered. How do you feel?"

I took one of her hands again, smiled again and replied, "In considerable pain, but everything seems attached and I should heal in time. Seeing you again makes the pain more than worth it."

She seemed reassured. The surgeon and nurse reached my cot. He nodded to my wife, and then pulled the bandages off my wound. This was excruciating. Maud stared at my injured shoulder. I feared she might become sick, so told her, "Best not to look at it." She shook her head, I wasn't sure why. The surgeon looked hard at the wound, sniffed it for signs of gangrene, evidently was reassured and told the nurse to bandage me again.

As she was doing this, the surgeon addressed Maud and me, "We are short of beds. So tomorrow if all goes well, you can leave the hospital and stay with your wife. Just come in each morning to have the wound checked and the dressing changed."

I was delighted, though sweaty and weak from the pain. Maud seemed much less happy, so I tried to reassure her, "I won't be any trouble, well, no more than usual."

She forced a smile. I could see she was shaken, not surprising. The surgeon moved off as the nurse finished. Maud stood up, clearly intending to leave. I kept hold of her hand and told her, "Two things I have to tell you before you leave. I was just promoted first lieutenant, which means a little more money. I haven't asked you about this, but do you have enough? I can arrange to have a bigger allowance paid you."

Maud seemed impatient, said, "No, David."

She seemed about to say more, but I interrupted her, "The other thing is a request. Please, dear, send a telegram to my family telling them I am in hospital here with a shoulder wound."

I was looking at her as I said this, saw she was forcing resignation on herself. "Of course, David, I will do that directly."

I released her hand, smiled again at her as she hurried away. I supposed she had a job she was late for. I saw admiring looks directed at her by some of the other patients. I lay back, tried to outwait the pain, tried to nap, tried, when I found I couldn't sleep, to think of entertainments to take my wife to, but for that I needed newspapers. In time as I relaxed more and more, I almost went into a trance-like state while hospital routine surged and ebbed, a few men leaving on their feet, usually assisted, many more being brought in.

Two meals and one trip to the loo later, visitors appeared: my stepmother and half-sister. They must have come directly on getting the telegram. Since it was in term, I didn't expect my father but was very pleased to see them both again. Rose was become quite the young lady and bent to kiss me. I smiled in response as she asked, "How are you feeling, Brother?"

My reply was, "Feeling guilty about lounging in luxury, occupying space needed by better or at least more severely injured men. The surgeon said he thought I should be able to go home tomorrow morning, just come in daily to have my bandages changed. Where are you staying?"

My step-mother was about to say something when my wife walked up. She was wearing one of her usual dresses and was carrying a box of Swiss chocolates, rather pricy things but I appreciated her thoughtfulness. The women exchanged greetings, found chairs and sat down. I managed to open the box of chocolates and offered them to my visitors before selecting one for myself. I couldn't remember having candy this good. My visitors liked it, too.

Maud asked them, "Where are you staying?"

My step-mother replied, "We will have to find a hotel, I suppose."

Maud said, "Come with me to my parents' flat. You can sleep in my brother's room as he is at sea."

This was again thoughtful and kind and I smiled at my wife, another chocolate in my mouth. Her smile in response was not full-souled but less constrained than this morning.

My step-mother said, "Very well then, Maud, we accept your kind offer and will help escort David to the flat."

I quipped, "And to keep me from sampling the pubs on the way, I expect."

The three women smiled and Maud said, "That above all."

I laughed, as did my step-mother and Rose. Maud was not normally what I would call a witty woman, nor was I known for bandying. My step-mother and Rose, who had had a long day of it, left shortly after with my wife.

Early the next morning my dressings were again changed and I was promoted to the status of occupant of a wheeled chair while I waited for them. I had been dressed by a nurse, rather embarrassing, so was in uniform. My bag was in my lap. I tried to make my mind go blank, just sit and breathe and heal. Even so, I was feeling impatient when the three women appeared, though by the clock it was still early. I gave Rose my bag and allowed my step-mother and wife to help me on my feet. I stood, assessing myself for dizziness, and then began to walk. I was able to proceed to the entrance of the hospital without really needing support but happy to have it. We booked a taxi and rode to Maud's family's flat in comfort. I kept hold of my wife's hand, every now and then turning to smile at her.

I said, "I think I would like to have a bath, then look at any correspondence. I have some money, so perhaps something a little out of the ordinary for supper?"

My wife gave me a brief smile and assented, "I will speak to Mother."

The bath was badly needed. I was able to soap and rinse myself, all but the shoulder,—most refreshing. My step-mother and half-sister had proceeded on to the train station after extracting a promise from Maud and myself to visit and stay the night. My half-sister said she would sleep on a cot in the pantry. I didn't know when this would occur, probably in about two weeks. While I was bathing, my wife came and went, on one occasion using the loo, still a little embarrassing to us both. I kept my eyes on the tap end, in part because I didn't want to become aroused. She asked me if my bathing was safe.

I replied, "As long as the dressing doesn't get wet, yes. I will need help drying and dressing, then you can be about your business."

Maud said, "There are a few letters, I think private matters. You can rest on our bed, after."

Wearing pyjamas, a dressing gown and slippers, I sat at the dining table and read and answered the letters. They were from friends, nearly all in the Army, every one telling me of men we knew who were gone. Maud had apparently been writing as well. I glimpsed a letter tucked into her purse with the return, "M. M." I briefly wondered whom she was writing to; her friends, women about her age, all lived nearby.

Mrs Millen's cook prepared a cheese sandwich and opened a bottle of beer. I wasn't sure I should be drinking this but I was damned thirsty. I finished the letters, the sandwich and the beer and went to lie down in the bed Maud and I shared, inhaling her scent. I was able to fall asleep.

Despite my request, dinner was in no way out of the ordinary, though I did justice to it. Maud was late, not surprising as end of the month, the busy time for her and her mother, was nearing. She told us of two additional shops that had booked their services.

I asked, "How many does that make total?"

Maud swallowed and replied, "We now do eight. We could do more, but not many more. So I have money enough, David. Living here, I don't need much."

That night we made love. Maud was doubtful but the pain in my shoulder was of very secondary importance. She seemed slow in responding, so I tried to focus on the pain to slow my own completion. I thought I managed to satisfy her, if only just. After we were silent; despite our lovemaking I felt her distance. I was going to ask her about this but fell asleep.

The next day, two events: Maud's monthly courses began, so I was just in time, though in the past, she had been more responsive then, not less. I was going to ask her about this, but hesitated. Then the second event: her brother appeared. Once again he had completed his voyage, no torpedoes. I gathered he was in line for his own ship, a cause for celebration, especially once it had actually happened.

At dinner that evening, he seemed expansive—for him I mean: actually he said as little as usual. After the meal, he actually proposed a trip to a pub; clearly he was in a very good mood. I readily agreed to accompany him: Maud was going to retire early and I was still hesitant to talk to her, I wasn't sure why.

However, I said to the others, "He needs to be accompanied by someone responsible." There was a pause, the others were mildly amused, then I added, "And I pledge to you all my best efforts to find such a person."

The others laughed, Maud included. I think she was surprised to find me capable of saying something witty, on purpose I mean. So her brother and I set out. He evidently had one particular pub in mind, where he was known of course. We settled into a small booth, a pint apiece before us.

We had each downed several when I was prompted to say, "I never seem to know what Maud is thinking."

He took a long pull at his pint, then replied, "I've never been able to fathom what Maud's thinking."

And that was the extent of our conversation, save for the occasional, "My round, then," from one or the other of us.

We returned late not surprisingly. I settled into bed next my wife as gently as I could, but she was awake or woke up when I lay down.

She complained, "You smell of beer and tobacco smoke."

I was taken aback, finally saying, "Do you want me to sleep somewhere else?"

She was silent, and I wondered where else I could sleep, but finally she said, "Just an observation, David. Did you have a good time?"

I thought, and then said, "Conversation was almost non-existent, but, yes, it was pleasant. I was able to safeguard your brother from all manner of temptations. Unfortunately, he performed the same service for me."

My wife commented, "My brother has never been one for chatter. It is hard for me to figure out what he is thinking."

I smiled in the darkness and said, "After I visit the hospital, I will have a bath."

"Have your clothes washed, too."

"Yes, my lady."

At this she was silent. I wondered if I had offended her somehow. Then I fell asleep.

The next day after my dressings were changed, I did as I was bidden. Mrs Millen good-naturedly agreed to have the clothes I was wearing last night washed. So wearing my other uniform, I went to get my second diamond. Also, I had been in service in the RAMC more than a year, so was entitled to wear a chevron on my sleeve, in fact a gold one since I had been wounded. For some reason, I wanted to impress my wife.

Returning from these errands, I encountered my first house monitor, David Threlfall. He actually recognized me as well, which flattered me. He was in uniform himself of course, a major though I didn't recognize his regimental badges. He naturally invited me to a pub and I was happy to accede, though still feeling some of the effects of last night's excursion.

Over a pint apiece, we brought each other up to date on our doings. We were both married; he had a son and had been a new-fledged barrister before the war began. He seemed impressed by my profession, and I assured him it was all the more impressive, given the limitations of my education, "University was a new intellectual world to me. I had to struggle."

He nodded and said, "Even I had trouble adjusting to the Inns of Court. I used to think a Classical education prepared one for anything, but my son is going to be educated differently. Any offspring of yours yet?"

I replied, "No. We agreed to postpone children until I was established. God only knows how long that will be."

Our conversation turned to mutual acquaintances, many still alive, some not. He said, "Your old nemesis Landrum is still above ground. I saw him a day or so ago, evidently on leave. Captain. Didn't see which regiment. We nodded to each other, that's all." Silence while we each drank then he resumed, "Never cared for the fellow, that's a fact. Understand he has digs in town and works in some charity. Gratis I think." I raised my eyebrows and he responded, "Something to do with street children, I've heard."

I took another drink and said, "Sounds commendable if expiatory."

David nodded; of course he had heard the story and our conversation moved on to better liked acquaintances. It was a very pleasant conversation overall; I had always like Threlfall, and for some reason he had liked me. We did not talk about the war.

Back at the Millen's, I took a nap. Maud wouldn't be back until evening, her brother was off somewhere and I had missed lunch. Mrs Millen was delighted to sew the gold chevrons on my uniforms. I had put the diamonds in myself.

Maud awakened me, saying, "Dinner is ready, David. Or aren't you hungry?"

I stretched and stood up. I replied, "I actually missed lunch, so yes, I am hungry. I met an old school chum, my first house monitor in fact, and we talked over a pint or two. Or three."

"What about?" she asked as we descended the stairs.

"Schoolmates," I said and thought her expression changed somehow, but her face was turned to the steps so I couldn't interpret it, not that her face was ever easy to read. She was silent as we went in to eat.

Three days later, Maud told me she was done temporarily with that month's books and we could visit my family as promised. My shoulder was healing, though still sore, and I thought I could make the trip. So, the following morning, we arose early, packed for a two days' trip and went by taxi to the station.

A VISIT

On the train, Maud was silent and once again I could not interpret her silence. For that matter, I hadn't much to say myself. It was still full light when we arrived. I had sent a telegram to warn my family, so we were expected and welcomed. As promised, Maud and I would share Rose's bed. The meal showed care in the preparation, no effort spared to show we were honoured guests. Maud began to smile and even to chatter. That was unusual but pleasing to me. So the visit at least began favourably.

The next morning, Maud and I went for a walk. The countryside was very much as I remembered it all my days: verdant and misty. A romantic landscape I thought. Inevitably, we walked down the lane below my ancestor's patch in the high meadow next to the "good man's croft." This time I could see birds flying about the croft, so there appeared to be animal life in the place after all.

I proposed we visit my ancestor's patch. I had spoken to Maud several times about the place and she seemed resigned to the walk up the hillside. So I climbed over the dry stone wall, reached across it, picked my wife up and swung her over the wall. I had not done that since our honeymoon, and the memory of that caused her to flush slightly. I even took the opportunity of our heads being close to steal a kiss.

"Really, sir," she said in reproof.

I replied, "Surely a man may kiss his own wife. I don't think the sheep will gossip."

Maud smiled and we started. I warned her to keep her eyes where she was stepping, as the ground was rough and decorated with droppings, some new and so slippery. Maud took my arm, she was uneasy about the sheep, and I told her to walk in my lee. My shoulder hurt some from lifting her over the wall, but I said nothing.

As we got closer to the place, her shoe threw a heel; and while I could knock the thing back onto her shoe, we couldn't be certain it would stay put on steep, rocky ground. So once more I picked her up and carried her the last hundred yards or so. My shoulder began to hurt in earnest, so I was glad to set her where I imagined my ancestors dwelt for so long. I showed her the stone circle, the spot in the centre where a fire had been. Not after all very impressive and indeed she was not very impressed. I think the "good man's croft" didn't impress her much either, just a patch of forest, birds flying about and nesting. I thought I saw a squirrel.

We began to return; my wife treading cautiously, her arm linked with mine. Once more, she seemed nervous about the sheep, though these mostly paid us little heed. The heel worked loose again and once more I slapped it back on, but it was clearly going to need the services of a cobbler. So braving the pain in my shoulder, I again picked my wife up, glad she was so light, and continued down the hill toward the dry stone wall. I was very careful about where I stepped, I certainly didn't want to fall, yet couldn't see my feet for my burden.

The pain in my shoulder had advanced beyond savage and I was sweating and weak and becoming faint by the time we reached the wall. I set Maud on the top, paused a minute or so to breathe and recover a bit, then climbed over the wall, once more picked Maud up and swung her safely onto the ground. She was concerned at my state, reached up with her handkerchief, dabbed my face and ask, "Are you all right, David?"

I tried, probably unsuccessfully, for insouciance as I said, "My shoulder hurts a bit. Actually a lot. But carrying you was something I enjoyed very much, otherwise."

We smiled at each other. Maud was evidently impressed by my hardihood and not insensitive to the romance of my efforts which made me happy.

Mercifully, the heel remained attached for the rest of the walk back, which after all was on relatively level ground. At my families' house, I set her in a chair and took both shoes to the cobbler, as she complained a sole was coming loose on the other shoe. The cobbler was willing to focus on my wife's shoes; so I returned to my family's house in less than an hour, my wife's footwear restored to service.

At the house, I found the conversation centred on the Landrums, which I did not like, yet could hardly object. Maud was curious about the family, their customs and behaviour, what sort of landlords they were, yet I suspected her real interest was in one particular Landrum. I began to sulk, and since my family was not really that interested in the Landrums, the subject died. That left the war and my observations.

Rose asked me, "Is front-line service so awful? Are the soldiers in the line risking death every moment?"

I sipped my tea and told her, "From what I hear, front-line service is simply a filthy, boring, wearying existence. There is danger, from enemy snipers for example, or unlucky artillery rounds, but the danger is small. The real danger is in attacks; there casualties are enormous, usually for little gain. I confess I am become very cynical about our generals. They do their best, but they simply haven't yet figured out how to successfully carry out an attack without very great losses. I do not see that situation changing very much very fast. I hope I am mistaken, but my views are becoming widely shared."

My wife and my family stared at me, a little stunned. My wife said, "So it will go on and on?"

I nodded. "Each side is expecting to outlast the other, so the answer to your question is 'yes'. No government that throws in the towel can expect to survive. One side or the other will win, though exactly what it will 'win' will probably very quickly be decided to be not worth the cost."

We were all silent, and then my stepmother roused and invited us to lunch.

My shoulder made eating awkward; Maud noted this and looked at me. I smiled at her in response, she smiled herself and the day brightened. After, she suggested we visit Dr Potter, which surprised me some. But we went.

Potter and his wife seemed glad to see me, surprising me further. However the conversation soon shifted to Potter's proposed retirement upon sale of his practice. He apparently thought I would replace him. Maud was clearly interested in living here after I got out of the Army. I had assumed she would want me to stay in or near London, near her family and business. However, I asked what he expected to get and how much the practice yielded.

"It brings in £350 a year, easy," he claimed.

This would be enough to live on and raise a family, so I was intrigued. Clearly, Maud was also favourably impressed.

"How much?" I asked.

"A thousand pounds," was Potter's reply.

Given the return, that was reasonable. If Maud kept the books and greeted the patients, we would be able to live reasonably well. There was a woman who served as nurse; she made £36 a year, which the practice would have to support, of course. Still, saving only the trifling detail of indefinite service in the RAMC, our future was becoming definite. Maud and I left, both pleased.

Walking back I asked my wife if she wanted to move here, away from her family and occupation.

Maud replied, "Whither thou goest, David. If we have children, I want them growing up in the country, not in London.

And I may be able to keep books for tradesmen here or in Cirencester once the children are old enough. And costs for things are likely less than in London, so we should do very well here. You have over £1,000 put by."

I nodded, commented, "With your bookkeeping business and my Army salary, we may be able to save enough more to buy a property. That would reduce our costs further."

Walking with my wife, I sensed we were in complete accord on this important matter. Our visit here was becoming more and more pleasant, sunshine and warm temperatures throughout. Only my shoulder remained outside the realm of happiness and love and that I could endure. The doctors would probably give me grief over the injury, but I could endure that also.

Back with my family, I found they also wanted me to locate here. My stepmother suggested one or two properties she thought were available and noted I was thoroughly familiar with the area and many of the patients, so taking over from Potter would be easy on everyone. A glow of approval surrounded me.

That night, Maud and I made love again, this time at her behest. She was clearly also very happy the way the visit was turning out. Returning on the train, despite the shoulder, I held Maud's hand, occasionally turning to her and smiling. The pain was more than worth it.

As I expected, the doctor who looked at my shoulder was very unhappy with me.

"What the Hell were you doing, Mendy? You know better."

I had some pulled stitches and the entire wound area was quite inflamed, though not septic; so I feigned contrition.

"I went for a walk with my wife and had to lift her across some dry stone walls."

That was a little economical with the truth, but he accepted what I said, grumbling that it set back my recovery and that my services were needed by King and Country. I nodded in turn, accepting his reproof, though I could see the casualty influx had eased, so retained an untroubled conscience.

The next few days, the pain in my shoulder slowly subsided and Maud and I attended a few events, including a music hall. Rather bawdy, no intellectual depth whatever, but that was what was desired. We both enjoyed it. When Maud went off to do or solicit business, I went for walks.

AN ENCOUNTER

The Millens' flat was in a marginal area, socially, but that was the nature of their business. I wandered through lower-class patches then increasingly I found myself in better streets. I was walking along such a street when I saw two men ahead. One, an Army officer, was inspecting his kit while the other, a stout "gentleman's gentleman" prepared a motor car. As I advanced, I recognized the officer: Landrum. His London digs were here. Almost at that moment, he looked up and saw me. His gaze shifted to my shoulder, though I didn't think the dressings under my tunic were that obvious, then looked directly at me.

After a fractional delay, Landrum said, "On leave, Mendy?"

I pointed at my shoulder, replied, "Blighty wound. Are you going back?"

I thought Landrum's servant disapproved of my informality, but I was damned if I was going to call Landrum, "My Lord."

Landrum nodded. I looked at his uniform. Captain, two silver chevrons, I saw that what I had taken for a decoration was just a regimental badge. No M.C., nothing very prestigious. Still, a serving officer. I hesitated then extended my hand. "Good luck then." Another hesitation, then he shook my hand briefly and, I fancied, insincerely. The manservant gave me a look which caused me to think of Dickens' description of a character that looked at others as though possessing knowledge to their disadvantage. The manservant got into the passenger's side; evidently Landrum was going to drive. I nodded to Landrum and continued my walk.

I heard the motor start. It occurred to me that Landrum's digs were not two miles from the Millens' place. This made me uneasy, but then everything about Peter Landrum made me uneasy when it didn't infuriate me. I began looking for the shops for which my wife kept the books; were they nearby? But if such were close, I didn't recognize them. I turned back, walking briskly as I wanted lunch.

At table everyone was silent. I glanced at Maud, who replied to my unasked question, "My brother has his ship. He leaves tomorrow morning for Southampton."

I looked at Maud's brother, asked, "Another pub visitation in the offing? I can schedule you for the evening, though it is short notice."

Her brother smiled, shook his head, said, "I leave early and want a clear head for my new command. After I return, though."

I saw the father and mother were conflicted: pride in their son's advancement, apprehension at the danger. The German U-boats were inflicting heavy losses on our shipping. As usual, Maud's face showed nothing.

Maud was working in her father's shop today, and there was nothing on anyway this afternoon, so I decided to take a nap. This should help me recover. I didn't ask what Maud's brother would be doing,—probably packing for his voyage. As I drifted off, an unwelcome thought surfaced: I fancied Landrum knew about my shoulder wound. This led to even less welcome thoughts: were he and Maud in communication? Given the complicity of the manservant, this would be easy to achieve. My wound may have interrupted something, at least temporarily.

I shook my head, trying to dispel these speculations. I kept telling myself I had no unequivocal reason to suspect Maud of anything, I had opportunities for liaisons with prostitutes for example. We had to trust each other. Eventually I went to sleep, my shoulder not complaining too much.

Awakened by my wife, I learned we were all to dine at a restaurant, a family favourite, before the son sailed. I was nothing loath, meals at the Millens were adequate but eating there every day tended to pall. The woman who cooked had the evening off, and so the five of us walked perhaps a half-mile to the place.

Some dishes were unavailable, a result of our shipping losses, and prices were sharply higher for the same reason. Still, we were all able to order something that sounded appealing, and the reality wasn't too much off. I think we all enjoyed what we were served. Maud and I exchanged a few things, so we would be more knowledgeable for the next visit. Unspoken was the realization we might never meet again.

That night after Maud and I had made love, she asked me where I had walked. I mentioned the streets and this time I had the distinct feeling she knew which street Landrum's place was on. I was driven to add, "I met Peter Landrum. He was going back after leave. I wished him good luck and we shook hands. He has an impressive motor."

Maud was silent a long time. I set myself to outwait her.

Eventually she said, "I know the street. I met him there once or twice on my visits to possible employers. I don't remember the motor. He had a manservant with him."

"I met the manservant. I think he expected me to be more deferential to his employer."

"You weren't rude to Landrum, were you?"

"No, of course not. But, perhaps presumptuously, I consider myself to be his peer. We attended the same grammar school and are both serving officers."

Maud objected, "You are in the Medical Corps not a front-line soldier."

She stopped, I think she felt she had said too much, but I was provoked to respond, "I've been wounded on active service; he has not, so again, I am his peer."

We were silent again. I could feel her anger. Well I was becoming angry myself. If my service wasn't fully as honourable as his, what service was? I remembered the awful conditions of my work, the exhaustion, the value of what I did and wondered how I could convey this to my wife. Or was she simply not to be convinced? The silence stretched. I clenched my teeth. I was not going to say anything more until she did.

I think she realized she had provoked me. Without conceding anything, she said, "I didn't mean to belittle your service, David, especially after seeing your shoulder that morning."

I was slightly mollified and responded, "What you saw was very tepid stuff compared with what is brought to me hour after hour, day after day."

My wife seemed relieved we were away from the topic of Peter Landrum. "I had a nightmare after seeing your shoulder."

I put my uninjured arm about her and said, "I am very sorry to have distressed you."

"Do you ever have nightmares from what you see and do? Sometimes you mutter and toss in your sleep."

I was once more tempted to preen, to try to raise my standing in my wife's eyes, but forced myself to be matter-of-fact:

"When I began my medical studies, I had to dissect—cut up—a cadaver, a corpse. This was to learn anatomy. We were warned that most students began to have nightmares after a few weeks of this. I did indeed have these. My work as an Army doctor exposes me to much worse as a matter of routine. So yes, I have nightmares nearly every night. I have heard that these fade once the constant exposure to such sights ends, but that sort of work is not something one ever gets used to. As long as I don't disturb your sleep, they are just another thing I must endure."

We fell silent now but at least were silent together, I mean companionably. I turned to her, kissed her forehead, and then drifted off.

Maud's brother left very early next morning. We all saw him off. I shook his hand; Maud embraced him, just as his parents did. Then he was gone. I wondered if my approaching departure would be as noticed. My shoulder was healing rapidly. In fact, the surgeon at the hospital began hinting I should devote some of my no doubt abundant spare time to helping at the hospital. I said I would talk to my wife; I saw he regarded this as unworthy of a man and professional, but I felt my time with her, however derived, was precious.

But Maud agreed with the surgeon, though saying I should limit work at the hospital to daytimes; that we would go out together in evenings. I didn't know if my being about all day was wearing on her, but had to agree. So I re-joined the hospital staff, assisting where I could as I could. After the carnage of the Somme, things were mercifully much quieter, enabling much more attention to be paid to the relatively small numbers now arriving.

True to her word, Maud and I sallied forth nearly every evening, for there were many entertainments. I guessed this was a response to the relentlessly grim tidings from the war and my wife agreed. Still, we took full advantage of the situation. My recovery time went quickly until the day I was "passed fit" and given orders to return to France in two days. These ebbed away.

Maud and I faced each other on the platform at the train station. She was composed, though her eyes were sad. I was glad to see that, but otherwise was loath to leave.

I told her, "With all the pain, it was more than worth it, enabling me to be with you again." I cleared my throat, hoping my emotions wouldn't get the better of me. "I shall miss you. The only good thing about my work is that it keeps me from constantly thinking about you. Please write often; when I am off duty, your letters will bring your dear form and face alive again. And I shall write to you then also, of course."

She was moved, I could see. We embraced and kissed. I said, "*À bientôt*", turned to my carriage, climbed in, turned back again, and looked out at her. We raised our hands and then the train pulled away. I set my things on the shelf and sat down. There were five or six others in the compartment. No one said anything; all, I supposed, thinking about loved ones left behind.

RETURN TO THE FRAY

I had been reassigned to the same sector, many of the same people, but our ADS was about four miles closer to Berlin. The additional ground we had to cover was completely torn up by shells and spades. Flickers of light from gunfire and shells exploding showed barbed wire everywhere, some still on posts, bits of kit, British and German, bodies and bits of bodies, also British and German, increasing numbers of white wooden crosses as the bodies were collected and buried. I saw many of the crosses had no name, and thought of the families, friends and sweethearts of these men, never knowing where their son, husband, or brother lay. I arrived at the ADS, thoroughly depressed.

The ADS was built much like the others I had inhabited. Also, same smells, same atmosphere. I was in charge, so relieved my predecessor to return the following evening as dawn was approaching. I checked over the men waiting to be taken back. These had mostly just been brought in, but one or two men were too seriously injured to be moved yet. I worked on these until I thought they could be taken to the CCS; the others had been competently patched up. I turned my attention to the tea supply. My recipe was still being employed, I was happy to see, so I distributed hard candies to everyone conscious. Then I napped, as there were a few cots open.

By contrast, my tour at the ADS dragged toward my relief. I supposed I was doing some good, yet everyone around me knew his business. Mostly, I presided, so had time to write a letter, a long letter to Maud. I described our situation, including the increasing problem with lice, regretted not only the work I had to do but the fact there wasn't enough to keep me focussed on that rather than upon her. I ended by reflecting that our time was so short, so precious that every moment of our lives should mean something, and that she meant more to me than anything else. While I had to earn a living, I needed to remember that was only a means to an end, the end being our happiness together.

I wrote another letter to my wife after returning to the CCS, as once more I had the time. I had sent this when a letter from her appeared. In it she said she missed me as well and asked if I could manage to be reassigned to a hospital in London, perhaps on rotation. I inquired about this and instead was told I would be reassigned to another sector where a new offensive was planned. This had to be kept very quiet, I was warned. So my next letter to my wife told her that, save for two week leaves every six months or so, I was trapped, like all the other soldiers here on both sides.

Rotation followed rotation. Maud's shipments of hard candies were most welcomed by patients and stretcher bearers alike, as I repeatedly informed her. The peppermint-flavoured ones were particularly popular, though she would also pack smaller amounts of other flavours for variety. All most thoughtful, and I began to count the days when I guessed my next leave would occur.

Otherwise I again fastened myself to the surgeons, assisted them in every way at every opportunity, likewise with the other doctors. I wanted to learn and this was the best way to do it. And, as I had mentioned to Maud, it kept my mind off our separation.

My colleagues were mainly a congenial bunch, which made all our duties easier. Every so often, when business was exceptionally slow, several of us would take a staff motor into Amiens and dine there. I had hoped French restaurants would prove superior to the ones Maud and I had endured in London, and happily this was the case. We had acquired a list of recommended places and agreed to try them all in turn.

The meals were a revelation: nothing extraordinary about the ingredients, no frogs or snails, yet the results were superb. The reputation the French had for good meals was, we agreed, merited. I described what we had eaten in my letters to Maud, suggesting our second honeymoon be taken in France.

I and my crew had returned from the ADS, filthy and lousy as usual, but were sent to the base hospital instead of the CCS. We were given the opportunity to clean ourselves, clothes and gear, and then I was summoned to see the chief. He bade me sit and told me:

"Mendy, the Army's new offensive will start in two days. For obvious reasons, we are sending reinforcements, including medical personnel, only at the last minute, in fact at night. Once you and your men get there, you will have to stay concealed until the offensive starts. Then you will advance with the second wave and set up an Advanced Dressing Station less than a mile behind the new front line. Deal with casualties until you are relieved. You will start your journey tonight. Any questions?"

I thought, and asked, "How much can I tell my men?"

"You can tell them what I told you, except for the destination: the Army's objective is called Messines Ridge."

I nodded and said, "Then we will prepare to leave tonight."

He nodded in turn and I stood up and was turning to leave when he remembered something, "I forgot to tell you that you have been promoted captain. Good luck."

I walked out, my feelings in conflict. Being promoted was most welcome; aside from the greater pay, I was now equal in rank to Landrum, though he might have been promoted since I had seen him, but I couldn't say this to Maud. Also, I had the responsibility for my men, perhaps leading them under fire. I didn't know how I would meet those responsibilities. I would, like a great many other men, find out soon. Again, I didn't want to tell my wife this.

After collecting my men and telling them what was in the offing, we began packing our gear, including extra tea, sugar and the candies, altogether quite a load, easily fifty pounds a man. Of course, soldiers advancing carried as much or more. I snatched the opportunity to write to Maud:

> *5 June, 1917*
>
> *My Dear*
>
> *I have just been told I have been promoted captain, so there will be more money coming in. Also, I and my men must advance with the second infantry attack in an offensive to begin shortly, set up an Advance Dressing Station, and treat wounded. This will be hazardous; if anything happens to me, you will get a captain's widow's pension. Also, the knowledge I died thinking of you.*
>
> *May we meet again,*
>
> *David*

I posted this and then we all boarded a lorry and began our journey. I had also gotten us stocked with extra bottles of cold tea and biscuits as I didn't entirely trust the Army commissariat. Occasionally we stopped, always concealed in trees or under camouflage nettings. Clearly, surprise was intended.

We arrived early the next morning. There were guides, I was relieved (and impressed), to see. We hauled our supplies and gear out of the lorry and, slightly staggering under the weight and awkwardness of our loads, moved to our destination.

We arrived as the east was beginning to lighten. Guns were firing, mostly ours, nothing like the Somme, rather desultory fire. The woods where we were to stay were reassuringly thick and we were easily able to conceal what we had brought as well as ourselves. We were all tired, so spread ground sheets and lay down on these to sleep. The offensive, I was told, would begin early morning next day. In the meantime, no fires, cold rations only.

Through the next day we slept, dozed, napped as the woods filled with troops and artillery batteries set up all around us. Shells were brought in, lorry-loads of them. I assumed sharp watch for German aeroplanes was being kept. Also, the Germans were entrenched on a low hill or ridge overlooking us so we all had to stay well hidden. Smokers had to stay behind trees or lorries.

The tension increased as it grew dark. It was surprising how wearing such waiting could be. More troops appeared. As it became full dark, these moved toward the German lines: they were the first wave. Our firing increased somewhat. No possibility of sleep now. Then, about three in the morning, our guns stopped. Silence, save for the sounds of nightingales. We waited. Waited. Suddenly, the ground rocked and shook. Earthquake, I thought. Then all our guns opened fire, and I realized our attack had begun.

The second wave troops began to move toward the German lines. I and my men gathered our gear and did the same. It seemed more awkward than before, yet we pressed ahead determinedly, just anxious to be moving, doing something. Out of the woods, into the British support entrenchments. Duckboards had been set so we could cross the trench. Ahead, pioneers were standing about, some smoking. They had cut our barbed wire so we could walk through. This is a well-organized operation, I thought.

Ahead, I could see Messines Ridge; it looked oddly serrated, broken toothed as it were. I could see our troops in the first wave swarming over the ridge, and realized we had carried it in one go! I saw a few walking wounded, ours, then some men in unfamiliar uniforms, reeling, some staggering, and realized these were German soldiers, prisoners. There seemed to be a great many of them.

Across our front-line trench we moved into what was no-man's-land, now ours, through gaps in the wire laid by both sides. We were moving uphill, very tired now, into the German positions, now also ours. Looking to my left and right, I could see huge craters stretching several miles either side. Pieces of what I had seen and felt suddenly assembled in my mind, and I realized this was a mining operation. We had successfully mined the German positions.

Officers with unfamiliar tabs, presumably staff officers, were ahead, directing. One of them told me, "Set up your station about a quarter-mile the far side of the ridge."

I nodded, turned to my crew and said, "Just another half-mile."

All very well, but now we had to cross the German line. I had my crew stop and rest while I scouted a way across. In the crater stretching to our left, I saw British and German troops working together, apparently trying to free Germans trapped in collapsed bunkers. I saw the easiest or rather less impossible way across was to skirt around the near edge of the crater not too far away. Other men from our second wave were cautiously working their way across there, cautiously as the soil was loose.

I returned to my men, we all resumed our burdens, and started across. Closer to the German front-line trench, we had to avoid strands of German barbed wire snatching at our boots and trouser legs. At the trench, we had to climb over a cascade of sandbags, all loose. Some of these had burst and some disintegrated when we stepped on them. We leaned to our right to put our hands on sandbags which were still stacked but continually threatened to slide into the crater themselves, taking us with them. And we were top heavy from what we carried.

Then we were in the German trench, firmer ground but also scattered with sandbags. Still leaning to our right, we climbed along another cascade of sandbags from the rear of the German front-line trench. The loosened bags kept bursting or sliding away from us as we tried to climb up, then we were climbing, or trying to climb, the loosened soil behind the sandbags. I kept glancing back at my men, who were labouring to follow me.

There was a tree root exposed above me; I grasped it, the tree held and I could pull myself to the top, now behind the German front-line fortifications. Once atop, on firm(er) ground, I reached down and helped my crew, one by one, to greater safety. Then we moved east toward the German second line trench. I could hear machine gun fire, so there was opposition, yet our way was clear.

There was a small grove of trees next to a sizeable hollow in the ground, perhaps from a large calibre shell, perhaps natural. However, it meant less digging, so I said to my men, "Here." There were groans of relief, with which I fully sympathized, and we put our things down and began to set up. We had to wash our hands with water from our bottles, then Dakins solution.

Despite all we had carried, we had no tent or cots or stoves. These would have to be brought as soon as the Medical Corps people in our rear knew where we were. In the meantime, wounded began to appear out of the ground as it were, stretcher bearers and walking wounded, mixed British and German. I didn't speak German, the modern foreign language taught at my school was French, yet we managed to communicate where necessary.

By now it was full light, and more and more men were brought or found their way to us. I had sent messages with several stretcher bearers to arrange for supplies to be sent us but it would be hours for that to occur. Otherwise, we worked very hard and our supplies that seemed so abundant when we were carrying them up shrank rapidly. And we were thirsty. And hungry. And very, very tired. Yet we had to continue.

Added to this, the Germans were countering more and more strongly, their artillery mostly hitting their own captured communication trenches. Shells were hitting near us as well. Our hollow afforded little protection even if we could lie down in it, and to do our jobs we had to be upright.

Some of our stretcher bearers had returned with some supplies, so we could keep treating wounded. Even more welcome, some RAMC reinforcements. I put them to work, relieved about half of my men, and told them to sleep for four hours. The relieved men lay down on stretchers; we still had no cots. I had to stay awake as I was in charge.

There was a roar and at the same time, something hit the top of my helmet, knocking me over. A German shell, a big one I thought, had hit nearby. I struggled to my feet. I could still see, could stand, and knew what was happening. I took off my helmet, saw a small dent in it, felt my head, and was relieved there was a

131

bump but no blood. I couldn't examine myself further as several of my men and some stretcher bearers were down. I went to one, placed a tourniquet on his leg as an artery was opened.

My uninjured and lightly injured crew focussed on our new spate of casualties, and then began sending those back, the more serious cases first. Despite our shelling, British casualties in greater and greater numbers were arriving as the German counterattack intensified. I heard someone say we were entrenching and would hold rather than advance further.

More supplies arrived, including some cots and a stove, most welcome as we could now begin making tea. I had that set up first. As I was drinking the first of the brew, a tap on my shoulder: I was relieved.

"Thank God," I said, told my relief about the situation, then went to a stretcher lying on the ground, lay down on it and, when I opened my eyes, it was morning.

The next day was spent treating casualties and digging out for the ADS. Pit props arrived, also canvas and sandbags. Less happily, some severely injured men arrived, men we had to treat in the open air while the ADS was being built. We had two crews so worked in shifts, around the clock. Rations were eaten while standing. Sleep snatched whenever possible. No possibility of bathing or shaving, not much of emptying bowels or bladders. Surely once our entrenchments were complete, the flow of casualties should ease.

The Germans continued to attack while all of us worked relentlessly. Our ADS began to look recognizable. Once under canvas, I began to feel more secure. This was irrational, as inside the ADS was almost as vulnerable and probably less sanitary than outside, but I was used to having a roof over me while I worked.

We had been there about ten days when everything quieted. We heard the Germans had withdrawn from the salients our advance into their line had created. This strengthened their line but still we had won an unquestioned victory. Better yet, my leave, the second, "healthy" leave, came.

ROTATIONS

---◆---

I managed to clean up at the base hospital then obtained a ride in the back of a lorry ferrying supplies. I slept on the floor of the bed of the lorry, uncomfortable but I was so tired. I dozed on the ship carrying men across the Channel to England, also on the train to London, arriving in the dark, early morning.

Maud awoke at my entrance.

"David. How long do you have?"

"Two weeks," I answered, bending down to kiss her. She did not seem very welcoming, but had just awakened. I began to undress, I was still tired. I asked, "How is your brother? All well here?"

Maud got up to pull my pyjamas out of a drawer. I put these on as she said, "He is well, I suppose. At least we haven't heard of any sinking. Ma and Pa are well. They were impressed by your being 'mentioned in dispatches.'"

I hadn't heard this, but told my wife, "I hope you were impressed as well. I really don't know what for, but I won't take issue with any official praise."

"I cut out the bit in the newspaper so you can read it."

I climbed into bed with her; she seemed a bit wary, but submitted to my caresses. I managed to get her far enough along so I was able to satisfy her even after I had been months away from her. After, she commented, "It always surprises me to hear you were in danger. I keep thinking you work well away from any fighting."

I was silent a moment, irritated by her comment, before replying, "I was knocked down by a shell fragment hitting the helmet I was wearing. If I hadn't been wearing it, I would be under the ground, with a white wooden cross marking the spot."

She noticed my irritation and turned to embrace me. I kissed her in response, and then we fell asleep in each other's arms.

We arose late the next morning as it was a Sunday. The older Millens did indeed seem impressed. I had brought some tinned rations back which pleased all the Millens present. Ma Millen began planning Sunday dinner, proposing to incorporate one of the tins of bully beef into it. Maud fetched the clipping and showed it me. My work treating wounded even under German shellfire was briefly praised. Still, it was an honour. But I really wanted my wife's respect.

We searched the papers for entertainments, discussed which we wanted to attend, and then compiled a list. I would need to obtain money tomorrow. Dinner was filling, nothing more, though the others seemed to think it gourmet fare. My dinning in France had spoiled me, though of course I said nothing. Maud and I retired early, to the accompaniment of knowing smiles from Ma and Pa Millen. Smiles which were justified.

Maud had time, so began working on my clothes, which needed some repair. I went to the bank I did my business with, and collected a considerable sum. I wanted to get another piece of jewellery for my wife. I always seemed to be trying to please her, yet I was feeling mildly celebratory.

Being in the Army during wartime meant one didn't need to worry about money. The Army provided the basics, so there was always money for what I once considered extravagances. I went to a large jewellery shop, clearly doing good business from the number of soldiers present, all spending freely. I knew what I wanted: a jewelled hummingbird pin, for I thought of Maud thus. I told the clerk what I was looking for. He foraged about in drawers then produced the item. It was very expensive but I had the money and bought it. I had a list of other things, purchased those and returned.

Maud had made considerable progress on my clothes. Smiling, I handed her the box with the pin. She opened the box, stared at the pin, looked at me and said, "David, this looks expensive. We should be saving money buy a property, you know that."

I bent and kissed her and replied, "Do you want me to take it back? My wife should have some nice things."

Maud hesitated, I thought she was going to tell me to return it, and then looked again at the pin, murmured, "It's so beautiful," and her eyes filled with tears.

This shook me. I had never seen her in tears before. I sat down next her and put my arm about her shoulders. She leaned her head against my shoulder. I kissed her forehead and she began to smile, finally saying,

"Don't you dare return it, David. I will wear it to the concert tomorrow night. Thank you, Dear. But we do need to save."

"I suppose that rules out a second honeymoon in France."

She shook her head, still smiling, and replied enigmatically, "We shall see."

Ma and Pa were very impressed by the pin and supported me. "David's right, Maud," Mrs Millen said. "It's only just you should have some nice things."

This, I felt, settled the matter, and my wife wore the pin with pride to the concert the next evening.

We again visited my family, looked at properties that were for sale, and asked about the prices. These seemed high; but since I had a war to participate in, hopefully to help win, we merely nodded and took our leave. We could almost afford to buy one, along with Potter's practice.

My leave drifted on. We once more took walks and went out to various entertainments nearly every night. At last, my leave ended. I stood relaxed and refreshed on the platform facing my wife. I told her, "This leave has been wonderful. I shall count the days, the hours, the minutes until we are together again. Thank you, dearest." Maud said nothing; merely embraced and kissed me, not perfunctorily but I thought wholeheartedly. So we parted.

Back as before to the Somme sector, I was told of another major offensive set in the Ypres region to begin soon. I and my men might have to serve there. In a sense this was an honour: recognition that we were considered tops, but I think we were all wary of such honours by now. I had to keep quiet about the business of course. In the meantime, we rotated. When on duty at the base hospital, we were able to dine in Amiens, sampling more of the restaurants on our list. Most enjoyable.

Our offensive began without my crew's participation. We were just moved to an ADS, and I think our superiors didn't want to move us back right away. So we continued as usual. In fact, we had to stay at the ADS for a prolonged period as other crews that would have relieved us were sent instead. Fortunately, we were able to keep up with the casualties. I set up pots of water outside the ADS to boil our clothing. We even managed to have baths using an abandoned stock tank not too far away.

The offensive wore on. We heard nothing officially and the newspapers' reports were distrusted. Gains were claimed, yet these seemed small, ominously like the Somme. We focussed on our own duties as the year advanced through the fall toward winter. Then finally we were relieved, after three months at the ADS. The crew relieving us came from the Ypres salient. It was now larger, but the stories we heard were ghastly: enormous casualties, men drowning in mud, an otherwise incomprehensible number with "no known grave", the surviving troops exhausted and bitter. Worse than the Somme, though that was hard to believe.

Back at the Casualty Clearing Station, the head of station was apologetic; "Tell your men we are sorry they had to stay at the Dressing Station so long, but we simply hadn't men to replace them, they were all serving at Passchendaele."

That was the first mention of the battle's name that I had heard, but I said, "I will tell them, Sir." Actually I was sure we were all glad we had missed it but of course didn't say so.

At the base hospital, there were more stories, all reinforcing what we had heard earlier. I wrote to my wife relating what we had heard. I told her I believed all of it, that I was coming to the conclusion that we needed better generals, especially at the top. I was aware this seemed presumptuous, but I had dealt with the consequences of one botched offensive (the Somme) and one well-executed one (Messines Ridge). I was now certain the commanding general made all the difference. I concluded that my next leave should begin soon, none too soon for me, though my own duties had been relatively easy ones.

Maud wrote back, saying that there was increasing talk about the casualties and how little had been gained, also about the conditions. She hoped Lloyd George could improve things; she had more confidence in him than in Asquith. She added that her brother's ship was still afloat and that sinkings were beginning to fall with the new convoy system and the help of the Americans. So perhaps there were grounds for hope if not optimism. She ended by asking me to bring more tinned meat, nothing about missing me.

The New Year 1918 arrived cold. We were pressed to keep our wounded warm; we began to encounter cases of frostbite, "trench foot" that we had to learn to treat. Then, rumours: a big German offensive, perhaps in the Somme sector. Cravenly, I hoped that wouldn't occur until I was on leave, but realized the chances of that were unfavourable. If we were serving in an ADS, we were for it. The troops also, of course, but like most men serving, I thought mostly about myself, my own situation. Then my third leave arrived.

London, like France, was cold. I arrived at the Millens mid-afternoon to find Maud was out on a job. I unloaded the ration tins, well received, and began working on my clothes waiting for Maud to return. This she did, well after dark. She seemed tired, also not very welcoming. This annoyed and unsettled me: what was amiss? When I asked her about this, she seemed confused, then apologized:

"I am sorry, David. Of course I am glad to see you. It is just that this day has been so long, the muddles in the books were so hard to deal with and I am hungry. Did you bring the tinned meat?"

Somewhat pacified, I said, "Yes, seven tins; all I could fit in my case. Your mother said she was going to have the cook fix a stew."

"Good. Let me go upstairs. I shall be down again directly."

So I waited, sewing a second chevron on my tunics, this time a silver one. I no longer looked an utter greenhorn. It was vanity, all vanity, but that was all the Army had to offer its soldiers. I hoped Maud was impressed.

If she was, it was not obvious. But she did submit to be kissed, and then sat down of the sofa and began assisting me. We worked together until called to dinner. Maud was indeed hungry, as was I, and we ate everything available. After finishing the sewing, we sat together on the sofa and talked as we had done during our courtship. Gradually she moved closer, I put my arm about her shoulders and we became friendlier.

After we had made love, I asked her how she was faring otherwise. She said, "It is cold this winter, bitter cold. I don't know how the men in the line stand it."

"Some of them don't. We have had cases of frostbite. Everyone is trying to stay warm. I hope I will be able to perform that service for you while on leave."

My wife put her arms around me and said, "It is good, having you back, David."

This admission reassured me and I smiled in response.

ON THE RUN

---◆---

Returning after my leave, I heard much more extensive and detailed stories about the German Spring Offensive. It was indeed aimed at the Somme sector, our sector. There was nothing we could do about it but worry. Near the front, at the ADS, it did seem ominously quiet: few casualties and those increasingly self-inflicted. This was very worrisome. I began to wonder what we could do if the Germans broke our line. If I was in charge of an ADS if that happened, we would either have to surrender or try to escape. Since care of the wounded was my primary responsibility, I couldn't run away, yet I was damned if I was going to let the Germans lock me in a cage for months or years.

I began to look around the countryside, trying to identify escape routes. We would have to go overland, probably at night, carrying our severely wounded. I made plans, laid in supplies including extra stocks of morphine, arranging for extra stretchers while struggling with feelings of hopelessness. Of course, if we were at the CCS or base hospital, we would be all right, two chances in three. Or if overwhelmed with casualties, no hope. I would have to stay with my crew and my wounded. I warned Maud of what might happen. I didn't really think our line would hold.

An additional complication was that the Germans would use gas. More stocks, this time of gas masks. Practice putting these on ourselves and on our patients, over and over again, including in the dark. My worries transmitted to my crew, but in a way that was good. More ground sheets, to wrap our wounded in.

Rotations back were met with relief. At the base hospital, I tried to learn all I could about treatment of gas cases: the best treatment was prevention, use of gas masks. So my exercises and precautions were worthwhile.

Rotation up to the ADS was filled with apprehension. My wife's letters were encouraging, telling me of rapidly increasing American support, that we were certain to win in the end; and that she would pray for me. This last greatly surprised me, for only once before had words on any religious topic been exchanged. Nor were her family churchgoers. Evidently my worries had affected her. She enjoined me not to try anything foolhardy, that she wanted me to survive; she didn't want to be a widow. Well, I didn't want that either.

At the ADS, I kept everyone busy with exercises since we had few casualties to deal with. I spent more time with some of my crew, plotting escape routes. If we could move at night, our chances would be much improved. We discussed tactics; some of my crew had useful suggestions.

Back to the CCS: apprehension was increasing. My superiors took the position that it was the Army's responsibility to keep the Germans out; that we in the RAMC shouldn't worry about such things. Rather disrespectfully, I began to think they would be far enough removed from the front that they could afford a cavalier attitude.

At the base hospital, I saw the place had been emptied of all save the most serious casualties. I wrote to Maud, trying to assume a cheerful note, matching hers. I hoped the German offensive would begin while we were at the base hospital. Her next letter arrived, telling me her brother was still safe and her parents were well. My step-mother also wrote, telling me of my father and my half-sister's doings. They were beginning to talk of a public school for her. All somewhat reassuring.

Our term at the base hospital ended without any move by the Germans. Cursing them as lazy sods, we returned to the ADS. The men we relieved decamped immediately, despite the nearing dawn; everyone was on edge. We settled in, took care of such casualties as were brought in, moved everyone out as soon as darkness fell, and waited. Looking out, I saw it was becoming very misty, good for us if we made a break for it.

No business at all, so I set up a rotation, one hour turns, while the rest of us slept. Knocked off my cot by a crushing roar: the German attack had started. I looked at my watch: 3:40. I ordered everyone into gas masks, and then went out to have a look: thick, flickering fog. Some men moving up the line took shelter with us. I distributed tea, told the sergeant of my fears and plans. He seemed inclined to be dismissive, though the German bombardment had sobered him. He and his men also put on gas masks.

I went out again. The air was thick with mist and shrapnel. I couldn't see very far, crouched near the ADS and waited. At length I decided no wounded men would be likely to arrive at least until the German bombardment eased. With that thought, I went back inside the ADS and ordered all lights extinguished, including the stove and any cigarettes. Then I went to the entrance of our ADS and again waited. I hoped I was being overly imaginative.

Some shadows, moving shadows: I strained my eyes, saw the shadows were soldiers, soldiers . . . wearing German helmets. They were moving toward us. I shrank back through the entrance of the ADS, whispered to everyone, "Germans! Get under the cots. Hide. No sound." With that, I crept behind and under a cot and waited.

Someone with an electric torch shone it into our ADS, the light flickered about, some words in German, and then the light went off. I waited, waited, tense with fear, finally decided the patrol was hardly likely to hang about, trying to catch some RAMC people. So I stood up and looked outside: perhaps lighter, the light still flickering, continuous explosions but farther to our rear. Then more shadows, more German soldiers, moving toward our rear. Armed. Our line was breached.

I went back inside, explained what I had seen and what I proposed we all do: escape, as any wounded British or Germans were now the responsibility of the Germans. So we gathered our things, including two or three stretchers as we might find some wounded, and moved out into the mist. We headed roughly northwest. I kept moving about my group, including the five soldiers, keeping us all together. On two occasions I thought I detected parties of men, almost certainly Germans, moving west. We cut behind them, eventually reaching some patchy woods. I and my crew had selected these for our first rendezvous.

By now it was definitely lighter; in fact the mist was clearing, so we concealed ourselves in the woods. From time to time I looked out. I saw larger and larger groups of Germans: at first infantry, then wagons and light field guns, all moving west. I could hear guns, some perhaps ours, so I hoped we were offering some resistance.

We lay flat, moving as little as possible, "doggo" as the infantry put it, concealed in brush, the entire day. Now German artillery appeared, setting up in plain view, and then opening fire. I saw several small groups of British prisoners being marched past. The uniforms looked clean, a very bad sign. At length more German infantry appeared, an enormous unbroken column headed toward Amiens and perhaps Paris. I felt sick, sick at our defeat, sick at the thought of having to overtake all those Germans, break through their line, then cross our own, assuming we had managed to establish one.

Blessed darkness: we could see gunfire to our west, clearly we were resisting. Shell bursts began to occur about the road the Germans were using, and about their artillery, sandbags rising about their guns. They had made considerable gains, but now were going to have to pay.

We moved west ourselves, trying to skirt groups of Germans encamped seemingly everywhere. My sergeant and his four men were armed, so we weren't totally helpless, but that was just to keep our spirits up. We could see a fire ahead, a large one, Germans swarming about one of our supply depots. Looking at them, I realized the Germans were not doing what they should, which was pursuing us, but plundering instead. That was the first good sign I had seen.

We moved around the depot. I figured the Germans would be focussed on what they could loot, not looking out for parties of refugees. Indeed some seemed to be gorging themselves, others drinking ration rum, loud talk and some singing. I saw no indication their officers were trying to get things under control, another good sign.

Dawn was at our backs and we were moving much more cautiously. We had seen no Germans at all for an hour or more. We began to descend toward a marshy stream when a challenge sounded, "Who goes there?"

Several of us replied at once, "British, goddamnit."

We waded across the stream and walked up the far bank. Entrenched on the top were our own, a most welcome sight indeed. An officer asked us, "Any Germans opposite?"

Gesturing to the east, I said, "We haven't seen any for some time. I think they are all still eating our rations and drinking our spirits."

We were allowed to continue our journey. I saw the men forming the defence were cavalry, their horses in orderly lines to the rear, another sign of the size of our defeat. Still, I and my party had escaped, so made for the base hospital as we had also lost the CCS in that sector.

I was rather proud of our exploit when I reported to the chief, a feeling immediately dashed by his accusation that we had run away, abandoning our wounded.

I was completely taken aback, protesting that we had no wounded to abandon, that I had sent back all we had before the German offensive, expecting a rush of wounded. All we saw, I insisted, were parties of German troops, there was no possibility of our receiving any of our wounded as the Germans had completely broken our line. I told him he could ask any of my men or, if they could be found, the sergeant and his four men.

He stared at me, I don't think he accepted my story, and finally told me the matter would be revisited, and to hold myself ready to answer further questions.

I was becoming indignant and said, "I am prepared to answer any further questions as I have done, completely and honestly." That ended the interview.

In the meantime, I worked at the base hospital. I was uncomfortably aware I was under scrutiny. My crew was assigned to other groups, we were broken up, and I was isolated. I fancied people were looking askance at me, isolating me further. I did not mention this in my letters to Maud, as I was ashamed, reluctant to reveal that I was suspected of cowardice.

After what seemed a considerable time, the deputy chief, a new man, summoned me to his office, a roughly constructed box, and told me, "All your men confirmed what you told the chief. But we understand there were a sergeant and four privates who were with you. What was the sergeant's name?"

I stared at him, trying to remember. When we reached British lines, we had separated after shaking hands. He had told me his name: there were three S's, Sergeant . . . Samuel . . . Stringfellow,—that was it. I told the deputy chief, "Stringfellow was his name, Sergeant Samuel Stringfellow. I didn't see his badges, but he was a Londoner, actually I think Seven Dials."

The deputy chief nodded, told me to return to work, which I did. At least I had managed to remember the fellow's name; I never learned the names of the four privates. I had no clue how long it would take to unearth, no, find the fellow.

More waiting, more work, but I began to feel a bit less a pariah, perhaps my imagination, but welcome. Letters from Maud appeared infrequently; my own letters were less frequent as well. I didn't know if I was going to be court-martialled or simply would be put back into my usual service, presumably with a new set of men.

Another summons by the deputy chief: this time he asked me to sit, so I realized the investigation must be over. He said, "Mendy, we located this Sergeant Stringfellow. He backed up your story. In fact, we were able to talk to two of the privates as well. So we are reassigning you to be in charge of an ADS."

For an instant I thought he was going to ask me not to run away again, but I fixed him with a narrowed-eye gaze and I think he realized such a remark, even in jest, wouldn't help matters. After a moment's silence, I replied, "I will leave directly, Sir." And I returned to service in an ADS with actual relief. I had been reinstated.

With a new group of men, things were a little awkward, but I tried to be unassuming and tactful. The tea I had made and the hard candies I could distribute helped a great deal. My work with the wounded established me, however. Here I felt confident, in control. I began to think of the men I had been pitched into the midst of as my crew and I think they began to feel the same way.

HONOURS

---◆---

However, we started to hear of yet another German offensive in the works. I tried to make preparations as I had before: obtaining extra stretchers, for example. I drilled my crew, putting gas masks on themselves and on our wounded. Some of our wounded objected, but I explained why we were doing this, and I secured their acceptance. With casualties being brought to us at a rate of several per hour, we were kept fairly busy just from that.

Rotation back to the CCS was a relief, even without fears of being engulfed by another German offensive. Having been pushed back so far, we were in countryside that was as yet unmarked by war. It was refreshing, when I had some leisure, to wander about. Otherwise, I made up arrears of correspondence with my wife, though I still couldn't bring myself to tell her of the investigation of my conduct.

At the base hospital, I felt more at ease. My purported dereliction of duty was, if not forgotten, at least unmentioned. In fact, I was included with several other doctors in making another trip, this time to Paris (Amiens was in German artillery range).

This was to check off another restaurant or two on another list. I had a very good time, since the cloud of suspicion about my conduct had finally been lifted.

My wife's letters seemed to form a pattern: periods when she wrote less often and wrote shorter letters, and periods when her letters were longer and warmer. I couldn't make much sense of this. Times when she seemed emotionally distant punctuated longer times when she was quite unhappy at our separation. During these latter, I tried to cheer her up by telling about the things we might do together. Otherwise, comments about the progress of the war, our prospects and occasional bits about her brother filled her letters.

Back at the ADS, I could see the crew we were to relieve were very glad to see us, leaving immediately even though it was getting light. We guessed the German offensive was expected any day, which focused us on our work and on gas mask drills. Casualties brought in were fewer, which might be consistent with an imminent offensive. We tried to move men out as soon as possible, and I asked the stretcher bearers to bring back extra stretchers. I told my crew we might have to serve as stretcher bearers ourselves if we had to leave.

One day passed, then a second. At least we had more time to sleep, fitful though it was.

It began early the morning of the third day. A crashing roar, continuous explosions of shells, some we could tell were gas, the ground trembling, occasionally jolting. I was up, went to rouse those asleep, though the cannonade had done that, we all had some tea, emptied bladders and bowels, donned gas masks, and waited. Every so often I would look out. This morning was clear. No custom as yet, though that should change once the bombardment had lifted. No traffic either direction. I couldn't tell if our guns were responding. I could see flares, rockets, presumably requests for artillery support, though I couldn't tell which side was sending up the flares. Probably both.

I went out once more. It was lighter, I thought I could see men coming back from the front, either bringing wounded or retreating. Whatever they were, it was dangerous. I fancied I could hear shrapnel whipping the air. Turning to our rear, I saw a cloud on the ground, colour a vague yellow-brown, and recognized it was gas. Then I felt a breeze from that direction, a morning breeze, and could see the cloud moving toward us. I went inside the ADS, warned every one that gas and perhaps wounded were approaching.

They arrived about the same time. A man on a stretcher with a deep gash in his side needed morphia as he was in great pain. I tore open his uniform, cleaned the wound, and had one of my men bandage it. I could have sewed him up right there, but he should be x-rayed first. The chest and internal organs were still enclosed, so I had the stretcher bearers take him back, as the German bombardment had lifted.

A man in distress: I changed his gas mask, and his breathing eased. I threw the defective one in a corner and worked on his leg, which was shattered. I hoped it could be saved; in case it could, after cleaning about the area and bandaging it, I had the leg roughly splinted. I waved the stretcher bearers to take him back as well.

A very bad head wound: pieces of his skull held on to his head by torn scalp, his brain exposed. I tried to clean skull fragments and exposed brain, uncertain whether I was helping or the reverse, but sepsis in the brain was certain to be fatal. I used my fingers to fit the pieces of skull back, and sewed the scalp to hold everything together, working around the gas mask. I sent him back too.

The gas masks were essential, but hindered communication. At times, we had to raise them up off our face to speak. Then we could smell the gas, so tried not to inhale, not always successfully. Some of us were coughing. I prayed we could all continue as the pace of casualties was picking up. Walking wounded began to appear. These were given tea and hard candy, quickly inspected and bandaged, and then they were sent on their way. If they requested it, they were allowed to rest on, or, increasingly, under a cot.

I managed to extract a shell splinter in a man's abdomen, checked carefully to try to see if the splinter had carried cloth into the wound, decided the splinter was sharp enough that such was unlikely, and sewed the man back up. More tea: this for the stretcher bearers, as they had a very hard job even without the gas and the shelling. I had to keep track of everything, simultaneously it seemed.

Now an officer appeared. He looked about, saw me, decided I was in charge, came over and said, "The Boche have broken through. Orders are to retreat."

I noticed he wasn't wearing his gas mask, removed mine, coughed and asked, "What about the gas?"

He was leaving but turned back and said, "Wind blew it away. Into the German's faces." Then he left.

I got as many of our wounded on stretchers and on their way to the CCS as I could, roused the men we thought could walk and sent them as well. The blanket that served as door opened again, I realized it was full daylight, and saw another man brought in. One side of his face was torn away, I suspect he was blinded. We could only bandage him and ask the stretcher bearers to take him on.

Some stretcher bearers appeared, thank God, and with them, I and my crew could take everyone in the ADS. We loaded ourselves with kit bags, bandages, disinfectants, everything we thought we might need. It was altogether a staggering load, but we managed to carry all our gear and our wounded out to join the retreat. Outside I didn't see many of our troops, then realized we were the last or nearly so.

On our way I could hear rifle and machine gun fire. Overhead we heard bullets whipping. We cringed but pressed on. Ahead was a railway embankment. I could see flashes from muzzles of rifles and saw this was our line of defence. At the embankment, we had to turn our stretchers parallel to the embankment. This was so we could lift our wounded on stretchers to the top then over, into safety, however temporary.

We made it over. Two of our stretchers bearers jerked, cursed but kept on. Examining them, I saw they were wounded, though not seriously enough to become stretcher-borne casualties themselves. So they became walking wounded. I sent them on, managing to recruit more stretcher bearers from lightly wounded men. The commanding officer wasn't pleased to see his strength further reduced, but I guessed he understood his stand at this place was going to be only temporary.

I felt I had to stay myself, partly to make up for this, and partly because I could see more seriously wounded men lying at the base of the embankment, men who needed treatment. So I asked my crew for volunteers to stay with me. Two volunteered and I sent the rest, mostly acting as stretcher bearers themselves, back after taking the medical supplies they were carrying.

We moved back and forth, crouched, at the base of the embankment, the lee side, away from the Germans. Enemy fire was increasing, more of our men were hit and soon we would be targets of enemy artillery. Some of our men had been killed instantly, shot through the head. I and my two assistants could do little more than bandage the others, after cleaning around the wound. I was able to give each man a piece of hard candy, which cheered them greatly.

Our numbers were shrinking. Looking west, all I could see was open fields, no cover. We would be hard pressed to get across these; all we could do was try to keep the Germans from overrunning us before dark. We had some of the light machine guns called Lewis guns but these weren't firing much and I realized we were probably running short of ammunition.

Some more stretcher bearers—brave men!—reached us and I selected the most serious, but salvable, cases to be sent back. They would have to carry their burdens crouched and even then were in danger of being hit, but off they went.

Our medical supplies were dwindling. I saw the commanding officer, a major, fall and moved to him. A neck wound, though no significant blood vessels were cut, so I was able to bandage him as he was lying against the embankment.

He said to me, "Good to have you here, doctor."

I replied, "A most interesting and exciting experience, Sir."

He said, "If we can hold on till dark, we can run for it then."

I nodded and moved to another wounded man.

I began checking the time. It would be hours until darkness. Our prospects did not appear favourable. However, for some reason the German fire began to lessen. Fewer casualties for the moment, so I could look for my gas mask. I had taken it off—somewhere—but eventually took a mask from a dead soldier. Also his water bottle, mine was empty.

Some of the walking wounded had sticks, and these went back crouched, leaning on their sticks. They left their bombs and ammunition, as we needed both, at least the ammunition. We and the Germans were now exchanging a desultory fire, and then even that stopped. Silence on this battlefield, though plenty of activity to the sides. We couldn't tell how things were to our flanks.

The light was going. I realized the sun had set. The major was talking to his sergeants. Approaching, I heard he was organizing a retreat. Some men would keep up a return fire to cover the retreat, assuming the Germans began firing on us.

Seeing me, he said, "We will try to take all our wounded. Organize that, will you?"

I nodded. He went on, "I don't even know your name."

I said, "David Mendy, Sir."

He extended his hand, "Ronald Whitchurch."

I shook his hand, and then went to find my two assistants.

Both were asleep. I realized I was well past exhaustion myself. Shaking them awake, I told them what we had to do. We had too few stretchers for men who couldn't walk, so had the less serious cases supported by two unwounded men. We assigned pairs of unwounded to each of these, with replacement pairs near, to rotate every fifteen minutes or so. We had stretcher bearers and replacements assigned to each of the stretcher cases. All that was needed was for the Germans to leave us alone.

It was well past ten when we began our retreat. I and my two assistants had to help with supporting and stretcher-bearing once again. Fortunately, our stocks of medical supplies were much less a burden, as they were mostly attached to wounded men. No German fire. Were they all asleep?

We crept over the open fields, into some scattered woods, crossed some fences, lifting our wounded over. Two of our wounded died; these were left where we discovered their death. Otherwise, this fractionally eased the lot of the rest of us, not that anyone felt better for that.

More fields, some with empty houses at their edges. The major, who was holding up very well despite his loss of blood, had us stop, and then sent one of the sergeants ahead to locate our line. The rest of us lay down on bare ground and promptly fell asleep.

Roused, I could see daylight approaching. The Germans were shelling in our rear, perhaps planning an attack on our abandoned position. The sergeant had returned with the news that our new line was about two miles away. So I and my assistants checked all our wounded, no more deaths, thank God, and we began to move, very stiff, damp, and very, very tired.

We crossed our line within the hour, were rewarded with food, drink, and fresh stretcher bearers to take our wounded to the ambulances. Then I and my two assistants found a ride in an empty ammunition wagon to the CCS.

I was happy to see a new chief surgeon at the CCS, not that anyone could rationally reproach me this time: we had retreated with all our wounded with the absolute rear-guard, no one possibly left behind. I had performed my duties under fire and I thought had performed them capably. Assuming that Major Whitchurch survived, he would surely vouch for me.

The chief seemed cordial, listened to my story, including my praise of my two assistants (and indirectly of myself), and told me to get some rest before resuming my duties. I relayed these instructions to my two assistants. We were all assigned cots, undressed and lay down for an actual sleep.

. . . I was struggling to stand upright on the slope of a crater, overladen, yet sliding inexorably down loose dirt toward the "good man's croft" at the bottom, the darkness at its base opened like a cavern, a maw, awaiting me. Above, Peter Landrum stood on firm ground, sneering at me. Beside him stood Maud, her hand outstretched to me but I couldn't reach it, I kept sliding away . . . .

It was dark; I was on a cot somewhere, sweating. I was afraid, actually afraid, to go back to sleep, I was so shaken by this nightmare. Then I remembered where I was. I got up, walked about, emptied my bladder in the bathroom at the end of the hall, and walked back, familiar scenes helping calm me. I could hear muffled groans and cries from other men, presumably also having nightmares. As I lay down again, I recalled a scrap of poetry or hymn from somewhere, sometime:

. . . who from the light doth swerve

Must ever darkness serve . . . .

I didn't want to think about that. It was too soon after the nightmare.

Over the next few days, the three of us caught up with meals, drink, bathing, shaves, clean clothes, and were reunited with my remaining crew, now at the base hospital. We would be sent together to set up a new ADS once our line was established. Otherwise, we were kept busy helping with casualties.

I wrote to my wife, telling her briefly of my adventures. A letter from her, written independently of mine, arrived. Her previous letter had seemed distant, but this one was warmer. I very much wished for leave, to enjoy this mood, but that was months away.

We were assigned to a CCS as they were swamped with wounded. Until dugouts and fortifications were completed, casualties would be high. We worked very hard, very long hours, yet without making much difference, it seemed. My stock of hard candies was exhausted and I wrote to my wife for more. Then I was summoned by the chief of the CCS. He bade me sit and told me, "A Major Whitchurch said you were invaluable to their defence, for which he was awarded a Military Cross. So you will be given a Meritorious Service Medal as well, for exemplary humanitarian service under fire. Congratulations." He shook my hand, clapped me on the shoulder, adding, "Well done, Mendy."

I was stunned, finally managing to ask about my two assistants who, I stressed, had volunteered and served under fire with me. He said they would be decorated also. He beamed at me, clearly my suspected transgressions had been forgiven if not forgotten, and I left the fellow's office, my elation and pride growing with each step. Now I had something to impress Maud with, my only problem being how I could acquaint her with it without appearing to boast.

As it turned out, my feats were reported in the newspapers, only briefly to be sure, but at least they had my name right. The decoration may have been a minor one but looked most impressive. My two crew men received Military Medals, which pleased them a great deal. Best of all, my wife saw the report and wrote me, saying how proud she was of me, but urging me not to take excessive risks: one medal was enough, she said. She actually added that she ached for my return, which aroused me and cheered me enormously. In celebration, once the candies Maud sent arrived, I made a general distribution, so happiness was universal among patients and staff alike.

Then we were sent to an ADS. The decor, the duties, the smells and the exhaustion all indistinguishable from our previous ADS residences. I had been assigned there to get things under control as the previous crew hadn't, yet I and my people were constantly struggling, control continually threatening to slip away. We longed for our sector to stabilize, to quiet, yet the Germans kept attacking and our line kept creeping back toward us. This was good for getting wounded to us faster but we began to think we might have to evacuate our ADS once again.

Back to the base hospital, a great relief despite the work. Another letter from my wife: her brother was engaged to marry, a great surprise to the rest of the family, including me. Who the woman was, when he had found the time to court her, all unexplained. Still I had to write a letter of congratulations and best wishes and did so. And I had a letter from Rose, good handwriting and well expressed. Not a great deal in the way of news, but welcome. My half-sister was also impressed by my fame, which she said had made a (small) stir in the two parishes.

A prolonged series of rotations followed. Now with hordes of fresh American troops and tanks as well, we were attacking. What was more, attacking successfully, gaining ground and German prisoners, though at great cost. Each time we returned to the line, the ADS had moved, toward Berlin, everyone said, though sardonically. Finally, some leave, though Maud seemed to have lapsed into one of her glacial periods, or so I gathered from her last letter.

I reached London in the middle of the night. I had slept on the trains, on the boat, everywhere it seemed yet was tired. I was able to get a taxi to the Millen's, awoke when the taxi driver shook me, paid him and let myself into the house. Upstairs, I walked into the bedroom Maud and I shared when I was at home. I had to turn on the light as it was pitch dark still. This woke my wife.

"David," she said.

"I believe so," I replied, bending to kiss her.

A tepid response to my kiss, then she asked, "How long do you have?"

I sat down on the side of the bed, began to unlace my boots as I said, "Two weeks. Is your brother married yet?"

Maud gathered the bedclothes about herself, either because she was cold or to protect herself from me, and told me, "I don't think a date for the ceremony has been set. My brother is in demand, and I think wants to make as much money as he can before the war ends. What happened to your tunic?"

"When I was helping carry a wounded man on a stretcher up an embankment we were defending, I felt something snatch at the back of my tunic. This was without touching me, fortunately. I sewed the tears myself." I had gotten up to get my pyjamas; I didn't tell my wife I had selected this tunic to wear home, hoping she would notice the tears and be impressed. So far, my scheme was working.

It continued to work. Maud was again a little distant but responsive enough so my homecoming at least began successfully. After, as she lay in my arms, she said, "This is my busy time, unfortunately, but we will have evenings. And nights." I smiled. For now, all was well in London town.

At breakfast in the morning, I again wore the mended tunic with the decoration and another chevron, my third. The Millens were impressed. More to the point, so was their daughter. I had quite a respectable display now, I hoped finally putting Landrum in the shade. I kept wondering if Maud's moods had something to do with him; was she seeing him? I feared to ask, yet the shadow of the fellow would appear, darkening my mood. For now, however, no evidence of divided feelings on my wife's part as she asked me to escort her to her first job of the day.

She had never requested me to do this before, and I asked her as we walked, arm in arm, if something was amiss.

My wife smiled and said, "No. Some of the shop girls are friends and are curious about you. I just want to show you off to them."

I was vastly flattered, but tried not to show it, just saying, "My exhibition fees are quite reasonable." Maud laughed, and I continued, "I will get papers to see what is on." My wife nodded.

As we walked, I reflected that this leave could hardly have begun better, which prompted the unwelcome corollary that it must therefore go worse. However, I decided I should just enjoy the moment, and did so.

I had brought the obligatory tins of bully beef—no stew available once more—so Mrs Millen and the Millen's cook could promise better meals. After displaying me, Maud dismissed me to buy newspapers and some items at a greengrocer's. This I did, and sat about the Millens the rest of the day, eating lunch with my wife, writing replies to letters from friends, venturing to the bank for currency for more purchases and excursions and taking occasional naps, for I was still tired. I hoped I wasn't coming down with anything, for the Spanish flu was spreading rapidly and I certainly didn't want to transmit it to Maud or her parents, yet when I woke later that afternoon, I felt much better.

That evening, after dinner, Maud and I went over the entertainments offered. We agreed on a short list of plays and musical performances we wanted to see. Also, in view of the spread of the flu, we would spend the money for box seats, so we would at least be alone. And we would go to bed early: evidently Maud was indeed very happy to have me back.

Despite the flu, despite the demands of Maud's clients, despite the shadow of the war, now turned successful, despite another shadow that would intrude into my mind at odd moments, my leave remained a most happy one. No encounters with Landrum. No mention of him by either of us. I hoped he was part of our past. Maud once more began talking about children, though again stressing the necessity of my being settled and established, with a sufficient income, before engendering any.

To this end, we again visited my family and wandered about, looking at properties. We saw two that seemed suitable: both cottages, both of two stories, yet the smaller one, priced at £400, seemed the better built and more comfortable, and my wife and I tentatively settled on that one, once I was free of the RAMC. We told my family of our inclination. My stepmother was sure we could get the place for £300. Maud and I looked at each other: that crystallized our decision. Our life together after the war ended was at last set and clear.

In one of our walks about the area, I proposed another visit to the high meadow where my ancestors had lived. I was thinking of how our last visit had turned out. However, Maud insisted she had no interest in such a visit, that we shouldn't be trespassing and that she didn't like the look of the "good man's croft." I thought the place looked as sinister as ever, even with birds flying about it on this occasion. In fact, she asked me to promise her that I wouldn't venture onto the place again. She seemed very much in earnest, so I promised her I would stay away from the high meadow. After all, there was little to see outside the croft and I was still unwilling to go into it.

We said our goodbyes on the station platform as before. We hoped and prayed that this leave would be the last, at least the last when fighting was going on. I told Maud, "It is hard to imagine life together, no separations looming, just day to day happiness, but I would surely like to experience such."

My wife said only, "Come back safe, David, and as soon as you can." We embraced. Holding my wife in my arms gave me a feeling of wholeness, of being complete. We parted once more.

Returning, I was given some additional responsibilities at a CCS. I suppose I should have been flattered, but I felt I had enough distinction. The extra work along with all the casualties we were taking, together with the added complication of the flu, made my life an even greater burden. At least I didn't contract the flu, though many of my colleagues did, leaving us shorter-handed.

No letter from Maud; I hadn't expected one so soon after I had left, though I had hopes of this, but day followed day with no word. I wondered if she had contracted the flu—did I bring that into her household? Or was there some other reason? The time stretched past a month, then five weeks. I had written two letters to her by then. At last, a letter from her.

It was as I had feared: she had taken the flu but had recovered. Her mother and father had then had it, so Maud had to see to the shop and care for her parents as well. Happily they were now on their feet once more. Maud said she hadn't been able to do the books of her clients, had missed a month but was working hard to catch up. She added that there had been many deaths, many, many more illnesses; that trade and life in general were disrupted, but she was glad I was still healthy.

Reading this, I felt guilt; had I infected them after all? I remembered my fatigue as I travelled to her home. Was that the flu, a mild case of it? I didn't know, couldn't know. So I wrote back to her as soon as I had two minutes for the task, saying I rejoiced she and her family were recovered, that I was well still despite constant exposure to flu cases, and that rumours of an Armistice were gathering and I prayed were well found.

FINIS BELLAE

They were indeed: we were told the guns that had hammered at the other side over 1400 days would fall silent; we hoped forever.

This was to happen at eleven Monday morning, the eleventh of November. Tragically, cases continued to be brought to us, some beyond our powers to help, until nearly that hour, indeed nearly that minute.

At that time and not a second earlier, there was silence. Then an enormous cheer, from everywhere it seemed, laughter and tears mixed, some dancing began. I distributed hard candies in honour of the occasion, was kissed by two of the nurses—another thing I wasn't going to tell Maud about—or would it prompt more affection from her?

From this point, saving injuries from German booby-traps, senseless, utterly senseless, we dealt with cases of flu. Even these seemed to be easing. Then we were told we would have to advance with the Army. I was put in charge of the preparations, another unwanted distinction. Since the Germans retreated very slowly,

159

we advanced very slowly, so I had ample time for the preparations. Consequently, our movements went smoothly.

This impressed my superiors. In fact, I was promoted major, very welcome indeed for the increased pay. What was more, the chief asked me if I wanted a job as staff doctor at a hospital in the northern suburbs of London. The pay was almost as much as Potter had said his practice brought in, I could set up a private practice on the side to supplement what the hospital paid and we would have nearly £1300 saved. This was partly from my pay but mostly what I had earned attesting recruits before joining the RAMC.

I was about to accept on the spot when I remembered the arrangements Maud and I had made, thinking we would move to Gloucestershire. I thought she might be happy to stay near her family, not excessively far from her clients, but decided to write, telling her of my promotion and prospects. I told my chief, "Let me write to my wife. We had made plans to move to Gloucestershire after I left the Army and I need to discuss this with her." I thought the chief was a bit scornful of a man who said he needed permission from a mere wife about a job, something surely entirely within the purview of a husband. However, he nodded and I went to write.

In addition, I wrote to Potter, saying I had been offered a staff position in a London hospital, so might not be able to buy his practice. I felt it was only fair to warn him of my possible change of plans. I posted both letters and went about such tasks as I had, feeling a trifle unsettled but overwhelmingly very happy indeed.

My wife wrote back immediately:

25 November, 1918

David

We had agreed to move to your home village after you got out of the Army. You also agreed to buy Potter's practice and we settled on a property we would buy. I understand this offer is advantageous in some ways, but I DO NOT WANT TO STAY IN LONDON. I am tired of the noise,

*the smells, the fogs; all the people crowded together, nothing
but pavement nearly everywhere. I want to live in your
village, with grass and trees and hills around me. Please
understand: I am very much in earnest about this.*

Maud

I stared at Maud's letter. She had never expressed such feelings so strongly to me before. I had no idea she felt the way she said. In effect, she had made some sort of ultimatum. I was a little resentful, very confused; but after working a few hours, I of course decided I would have to turn down my chief's offer. So, reluctantly, I did, clearly lowering myself further in his estimate. I then wrote to Maud:

28 November, 1918

My dear wife

I did not know you felt so adamant about this. Since you really want to get away from London, why then so we shall. I turned down the offer this morning, at your insistence. I will write to the estate agent, confirming that we are interested in buying the property, but for £300.

I have no idea when I will return: my services are much in demand, even as yours are.

Your husband
David

I posted this, and then remembered Maud's remark to me once: "Whither thou goest, David." This was disillusioning. And she hadn't said anything about the promotion. My happiness after the job offer had been turned upside down. I went about my duties, disconsolate.

A letter from Potter: sighing, I opened that. Rather to my surprise, Potter cut the price of his practice, to £800. He seemed very anxious to sell out, and I wondered: didn't he have any other offers? If the practice was as remunerative as he had said, there must be people interested. Once more, I wrote to my wife, telling her about Potter's offer. I didn't want to take advantage of the fellow. I asked Maud for her advice.

Again, a fast response:

> *6 December, 1918*
>
> *My dear husband,*
>
> *I ask your pardon for my peremptory* [Maud's first three attempts at spelling this word were crossed out] *tone. It was a good offer and I do appreciate your thoughtfulness at consulting me. Many men wouldn't have done so. I do indeed want to live in Gloucestershire, look forward to that very much and very much want to live in the home we agreed to buy. Mother showed me the notice of your promotion in the newspaper and I am embarrassed I overlooked that piece of good news in your letter. I am very proud of you.*
>
> *As far as Potter's offer is concerned, take it. I understand your scruples, but as I once reminded you, whatever you received from him you more than earned. If he is willing to lower the price of his practice, you must assume he knows his own business best. It gives us a bigger reserve, which we will surely need.*
>
> *Your wife*
> *Maud*

So the rift was healed. That was good, but left me uneasy. I had expected, not necessarily more deference, but more . . . love, more affection, more trust from her. However, I wrote to Potter, telling him I accepted his lower price for his practice, that I had been genuinely interested in the other offer, but that my wife very much wanted to relocate to Gloucestershire. I ended by saying I thought I would be several months more in the Army but would try to let him know when I would return.

In my dreams now, memories of patients intermingled with memories of Maud when we visited the "good man's croft," terrifying monsters issuing from the croft, monsters I was trying to protect my wife from, yet she seemed to be encouraging them, welcoming them, at which point I would awaken shaking and sweating. What in Hell did that mean? I went back to sleep, reluctantly, but I was tired.

Another distinction: I was now the deputy chief of my section. Though I boasted (discretely) to Maud about this, I wasn't paid any more and wound up doing all the actual work. Several of the doctors senior to me had managed to be sent home, hence my elevation. The chief apparently had no family except the RAMC, so was happy to remain. Especially since I was his dogsbody.

We would move every three or four days. The sappers were rebuilding the roads, railways and bridges, so we had accidents to treat, also flu cases, a scattering of diseases such as hernias, but there really wasn't much of a medical character to do. As we proceeded to Cologne, everyone became increasingly confident the Armistice would hold, the war was over, and the desire of us all to go home became obsessive. Anyone with connections used them to return. Though I kept busy, I grew restive and resentful. I could see myself marooned in Germany for months if not a year or more.

My exchanges with my wife stayed warm into the new year. I would have leave near the end of March and very much looked forward to that. Then another ice age developed. Her letters again became much shorter, rarer and more distant. By now we were in the Cologne bridgehead, and I tried to regale her with my observations: Maud had never been abroad and had occasionally expressed interest in traveling.

Cologne itself was interesting as it was quite different from London. The centre of Cologne sat on a semicircle of hills facing the Rhine. There was an enormous cathedral there and many very old buildings, everything soot-coloured from coal smoke. However, there was not so much smoke now, a result of one of the privations of this war, so the air was cleaner. Not as much noise either, as British Army motors were almost the only ones moving. Shops and dwellings were neater, not as much rubbish. Still, the greatest difference was the shop and street signs, all in German, of course, but giving the place the charm, the unfamiliarity of a foreign city.

The Germans were reserved at first. We were, after all, occupiers, victors, and they were the vanquished. Because of our blockade, everyone looked pinched. We were under strict orders, frequently reiterated, not to provide the Germans with food, and I suppose these orders were obeyed, at least when very superior officers were watching. Otherwise, the basic good nature of the British soldiers caused massive and unexplained losses of rations. These were often investigated but with inconclusive results.

I wanted to sample German cuisine, but the restaurants were closed. Not much business medically, good otherwise, but making our occupation tedious. I spent considerable time, wandering about. I always carried a few tins, only bully beef (the stew was too well-liked to share). I would hand these out to especially famished-looking people, especially children.

My leave arrived unexpectedly. What was vastly better, I was told I was to be furloughed, subject to recall if necessary, but I was going home for good at last. Our entire section was sent home, in fact, everyone laughing and cheering each kilometre marker until it grew too dark to see them. In contrast to my last trip home, I stayed awake, all of us talking and telling stories. I reached Maud's family's place early morning, though full light.

20

A RUPTURE

She was on her way out. She was dressed in the expensive grey silk dress with blue trim I had seen once before, when she had come to the hospital after I had been wounded. Again, it reminded me of something I had seen long before, but once more she seemed unsettled at my unexpected appearance. In fact, she seemed angry, telling me I should have warned her, by telegraph.

Staring at her as she told me this, I noticed something else: she had cut her hair short. This made her look almost boyish, from the neck up. Maud and her mother were not voluptuous, but had distinctly womanly figures. Maud's dress seemed to minimize this, increasing her boyish look.

Observing what I was looking at, my wife said, defensively, "It is much more practical, easier to clean and manage."

I said, "I don't like it." It just came out. I was becoming angry at her coldness.

In turn, her face flushed, and she retorted, "Damn you, David, I will cut my hair and dress as I choose. Do you understand?"

I replied sarcastically, "So glad you are back, David. Welcome home, dearest. I am so happy to see you home at last."

She opened her mouth, seemed to be grasping for something to say, probably something cutting, but I forestalled her by turning on my heel and walking out the door carrying my suitcase and kit bag.

Outside, I began walking rapidly away. Soon I found an un-booked taxi and secured it for a trip to the train station. As I was walking, some part of me hoped Maud would call me back, apologize, perhaps explain and my homecoming could proceed. Nothing of the sort happened, and I sat in a train compartment filled with other passengers, but alone.

As we travelled, I groped for explanations for her behaviour. She was clearly on her way to see or do something pleasurable and exciting, something I would impede or prevent. I remembered conversations with one of my medical school pals. He had been in love with a girl who led him quite a dance before their romance ended. She blew hot or rather warm, then when he responded to what he took to be her invitation, she turned cold. Eventually he had seen her with another woman. He had realized she was a Sapphic, she was interested sexually in other women but perhaps, we had concluded, she didn't want to admit this to him or to herself. Hence her behaviour. Was Maud actually a Sapphic?

Reviewing the years, interrupted years to be sure, that we had been together, I couldn't believe this. Which left only one explanation: she loved another man, almost certainly Peter Landrum, Lord Peter Landrum. That fit all the facts much better: the episodes of Maud's coldness could easily be from Landrum's being on leave or reassigned to England. In his absence, when I held the field, my wife would warm to me. She was clearly fond of me and enjoyed life with me, at least eventually.

An even less welcome thought: Maud's insistence we move to Gloucestershire must have stemmed from some understanding, some arrangement with Landrum. There, she would be close to his families' seat . . . but Landrum was living in London. However, he could of course always move back there. Why the Hell, with all the hundreds of thousands of widows, women who had lost fiancés, sweethearts or just the possibility of having someone, did that bastard have to move into my marriage? Was he that driven to best me in this? Why?

I exited the train, thoroughly unhappy, most distressed. I made my way to my family's place. I would stay there because it represented sanctuary, refuge. Once more, I would displace my half-sister but only for a day or so: I had my book of cheques, and would buy Potter's practice and the cottage Maud and I had decided to buy. I would begin my life as a country doctor; perhaps having to stay busy would salve my heartbreak.

My family were delighted to see me, quite a different reception from that afforded by my wife. Her absence was of course noticed and questioned. I replied, honestly, that affairs (perhaps in the French sense) kept her in London. I think my stepmother guessed something was wrong, but did not press the matter. At least not then.

It was after dinner that my stepmother cornered me outside, near the rose trellis. She said, "David, you are very unhappy about something, I suspect something involving your wife. Did you quarrel?"

I was silent, staring out at the countryside. Finally I replied, "Yes, I arrived home unexpectedly, she was dressed to go somewhere, somewhere she didn't want me knowing about. I strongly suspect she has been unfaithful, that her affections are alienated."

I was going to say who I thought she was in love with, but the heir to the Landrum estates was considered a very important person indeed locally, and if I was mistaken, such a speculation could be considered slanderous.

My stepmother put her hand on my sleeve and said, "David, I am so sorry. I know you love her very much. Just the way you looked at her told me that. And I thought she was very fond of you."

I commented, "She was—when I was there. When I was away, the other fellow moved in, I think. It will pass, I am sure. I will have plenty of work to keep my mind occupied." My stepmother smiled and we went inside.

The next day, I very quickly spent the bulk of the money I had worked so long and hard to obtain. As my stepmother had suggested, I was able to buy the cottage for £300. Also, the cottage was sufficiently furnished to enable me to move in at once. After unpacking, I hung up my uniform, with its badges, medals and insignia of rank, all hard-won, yet to no avail in a sense, as I was by myself. I put on my doctor's costume. Then I went to Potter's surgery. He was surprised to see me but delighted, especially when I wrote the cheque and handed it to him. I thought he was going to break into a dance, but instead he turned and walked out the door, leaving me with a roomful of patients.

I announced to the nurse and the patients that I had taken over the practice from Dr Potter, that I was from the village (which most of them knew) and that I was Dr Mendy (which again, most of them knew). Then I began to see the patients, sent in to the examination room, in order by the nurse.

The reasons most of them were there were either already known to me or obvious, so I simply continued their treatments. I assumed the nurse would collect the fees, also see to the books. Two other patients were being treated inappropriately, I thought. But when I prescribed different treatments, with different medicines, they objected. However, here I held firm, telling them they had hired me for my knowledge and experience and consequent judgement, and they should follow my prescriptions. They may not have been convinced but were certainly cowed.

A long day and it was going to get longer. Once the last patient had been seen it was past sunset and I was ready to eat at my family's place and especially sleep. However, the nurse, who also looked tired and unhappy into the bargain, told me she wanted to talk to me about something. I waved her to the chair used by my patients and sat heavily down myself.

"What is on your mind?" I asked her.

She seemed reluctant to speak but finally told me she had not been paid for the last three months and of course needed the money for rent and food, for which she was in arrears.

I stared, finally asking her, "How much?"

She replied, "Ten pound, total."

I thought, decided from her obvious embarrassment she was telling the truth, and brought out my notecase and extracted two fivers. I handed these to her. She seemed grateful, but I was shaken by the fact that Potter would do such a thing.

But there was more: she handed me a letter, addressed to Potter, from a medical supplier. She told me it had been sitting on Potter's (now my) desk for a month, unopened. By this time very apprehensive, I opened the thing. It was as I feared: it was a bill, overdue by several months, for medical supplies, over £45.

I looked up at her and said, "I will write a cheque for this directly, along with a note that I have purchased the practice." I continued to look at her then asked, "Have your wages fallen into arrears before?"

She shook her head, said, "First time, this."

I sat, thinking. She was making £36 a year, and I knew she was capable—perhaps more capable than Potter. And costs of things had gone up. So I told her, "I will pay you £4 a month, from now. Tell me, you do collect the fees and keep the books, don't you?"

She was very pleased, but shook her head, a sick weight settled in my stomach, and she told me, "No, doctor, Potter do all that. Never see a penny piece, me."

This was bad: I had lost a day's fees through ignorance, ignorance and trust, for Potter should have given me all this information, besides paying his bills. However, I had to press on, though I had a very good, or rather very bad, idea of the situation. "Where are Potter's books kept, do you know?"

She shook her head; I doubted Potter had thrown them away, though that was possible, so they were probably at his lodgings. Of course, if his rent had not been paid for months—since I had told him I would buy his practice, I guessed—I would almost certainly be expected to pay those arrears as well before I could get my hands on them. I looked at the wall clock, shook myself and told the nurse, "Well, now I have a clearer idea of the situation, things should go better." I forced a smile at her, she smiled back, rose and we left together.

At dinner at my family's, I told them of my day's experiences. They were angered at Potter's behaviour, though my stepmother claimed not to be surprised. She went on to tell me she had spoken to a village woman, whose name I dimly recalled, about service as housekeeper-cook at my cottage. This was helpful, and I thanked her. So I walked back to my place in a fractionally better state of mind.

I had never paid much attention to the actual payments of fees to Potter; certainly I wasn't sure how much to charge. Potter's books—he must have kept books, I kept assuring myself—should give me the information I needed. I set my alarm clock, changed into pyjamas, thought briefly about Maud, wondering if I would ever see her again, and slept.

Over the next three days, I met with many of my patients. I managed to find out how much Potter charged them by simply asking them. Most were forthcoming and most paid. I found a large glass jar in a dustbin. It was intact and I began putting the day's earnings into it when I returned in the evenings. I began keeping records myself on sheets of paper.

One evening I went to where Potter and his wife had lodged, told the landlord who I was and what I wanted. He told me he had some things Potter had left—"scarpered off" was how he put it—and I could look through them to see if I could find what I needed. As he told me this, I knew I would again have to settle Potter's arrears before I could take his books, but I was by now prepared for that. So I looked into a box with the things Potter left and, thank God, found his accounts, several books of them. One of the account books was about a third full and looking at the dates, I saw that was the latest. I told the landlord these books were what I needed, and he told me how much Potter owed when he left, about £5. I paid this, and the landlord informed me that Potter and his wife had left debts at several shops, but I hardened my heart toward those shopkeepers.

I returned, not exactly triumphant, but relieved, with the books. My new housekeeper-cook had a meal ready for me, for which I was grateful. After eating it, I tried to make sense of the books, but it had been another long day and I was tired. So I went early to bed.

Around midnight, the housekeeper-cook woke me up: a patient needed my services at once. A man, I assumed it was the husband or father, had been hammering on the door after repeatedly pulling at the bell. The housekeeper-cook had answered as I was comatose. So I quickly dressed and went with him to his lodging. A case of the flu: I checked the child's temperature and breathing and told the parents to keep the child covered, with plenty of water handy, and the child should recover. Both husband and wife were disappointed: they thought I should have some miraculous drug for the patient. I assured them that most people survived the flu, that I had a great deal of experience dealing with flu cases. I pacified them by promising them I would call in the morning. Then I returned to my cottage and my bed, remembering that Potter himself almost never went to see patients after hours, or so my patients told me. I feared I might suffer many broken nights, once my willingness to attend patients at night and on Sundays became known. However, I felt that was part of my duty as a doctor.

The next day I went on rounds, visiting patients in the other parish. On the way back, I passed my ancestral home and the "good man's croft." Birds this time. Otherwise the misty air of early morning made everything indistinct and hence romantic. I thought again about my wife, and then shook my head to try to dispel such thoughts, without much success. Perhaps keeping busy was the answer, in which case my happiness was assured.

Between the two parishes, my practice had plenty of patients though many were poor. Some had nothing to live on save the old age pension. These I felt obliged to charge less, say sixpence a visit instead of half a crown. Curiously, these always insisted on paying: it was a matter of pride. It was some of the better-off patients I had trouble getting to pay.

Two or three more dunning letters, fortunately not for very much money, but my irritation with Potter was now intense. The fellow was a damned bandit. Otherwise I collected fees from some of my patients, most of them, really. The others I was willing to let pay later, though I began to pay more attention to my own records of patients' payments. And I was roused at night two or three times for emergencies, or so the patients in question believed. I was still unable to muster the mental energy to try to make sense of Potter's accounts.

Once more, a late meal. The housekeeper-cook had heated some tinned soup and made toast, so I would manage to stay afoot another day. She also prepared breakfast and made sandwiches and tea for my lunches. As a result, I could keep at work with minimal breaks. It was almost like being in the Army again except the injuries were usually much less severe. I had been here in Gloucestershire now ten days or so, with no word from my wife.

I told myself I really needed to look carefully at Potter's accounts, so after eating I sat down on the sofa with his latest accounts book. I was tired, as always seemed to be the case, but opened the book and began looking at the records of the last month. Then a pull at the bell. I cursed—quietly, not to offend the housekeeper-cook—and struggled to my feet. Another patient, probably just needing reassurance.

21

CHEATED

---◆---

I opened the door and saw Maud standing on the step, two suitcases next to her. I stared.

Finally, my wife said, "Yes, David, it is your wife. May I come in?"

I stood aside for her, then saw her pause once through the door and look at me and I realized she expected me to bring her suitcases in. I did so, walked heavily to the kitchen and poured a mug of tea for my wife.

She sat down on the sofa, as did I, and she looked at me.

She observed, "You look tired, David, and thinner. Have you been eating?"

I replied, "I engaged a woman as housekeeper-cook. My hours are irregular and mostly late but she has done a good job feeding me. It is just that I seem to be on my feet so much, even when seeing patients in my surgery."

Maud looked at the accounts book and raised her eyebrows questioningly.

I replied, "This is Potter's latest accounts book. I have just started looking at it, I have been so busy."

Maud said, after drinking some tea, "Let me deal with that. I am the experienced bookkeeper after all."

We looked at each other and I handed the accounts book to her.

Silence while my wife drank some more tea, then she sat the mug on a small table next to the sofa and turned to me.

She said, "David, I apologize for my reception of you last week. You caught me by surprise and you know I don't like surprises. I was feeling irritable into the bargain and we quarrelled. I don't blame you for walking out. I blame myself for provoking you. I am very sorry and ask your pardon."

A jumble of thoughts coursed through my head: I was going to ask her whether she had been seeing Landrum or some other man, but I was tired and, most of all, I had missed her, more than I had realized.

I forced a smile and told her, "Only if you forgive me for my behaviour."

She smiled, was that a triumphant smile, I couldn't be certain, only that my wife had come to our new home seeking reconciliation. And that night we completed the reconciliation.

The next morning over breakfast, I told Maud about Potter's behaviour. I added that every day I wondered what new examples would come to light of the fellow's cheating.

I said, "One of the reasons I have been avoiding looking at his accounts is fear of what I might find. Otherwise, I have just been too busy."

Maud looked serious and told me, "I will spend the day looking through these. So you don't have to worry about them."

We exchanged smiles, I rose and kissed my wife and went to my surgery.

I didn't ask my wife about her London bookkeeping job. I assumed Mrs Millen now did it all, perhaps with some help. In one of her letters, Maud mentioned a young woman who was helping her and her mother. I wasn't concerned about this, just delighted to have my wife with me again.

That evening, late, always late, I came home—with my wife now in residence, it was that—and emptied the day's collection into the jar. Maud was sitting at the dining table with Potter's accounts books before her. The housekeeper-cook brought me dinner as soon as I sat down and I ate quickly as I was hungry. After I finished, I felt better, which feeling disappeared when I caught the expression on my wife's face.

I forced myself to ask, "What now?"

Maud's face showed a mixture of pity and, yes, contempt as she replied, "David, Potter claimed the practice brought in £350 a year or more, didn't he?"

I said, "Yes. You were there too."

Maud said, "But you didn't check his claim, just took him at his word."

I protested, "I couldn't check his claim without access to those," gesturing toward the accounts books, "and I am certain he wouldn't have let me look at them. And remember, you also accepted his statement and insisted we come here."

For a moment, she looked angry, then composed her face before telling me, "From his records, the practice brings in less than half what he claimed. David, he has cheated you."

I sat at the table after absorbing this. In a way, given Potter's behaviour in smaller matters, this revelation was not a complete surprise. However, with what I had to pay the nurse and the housekeeper-cook, we had barely enough to get by on, even without having to pay rent. This was more than depressing, it was shattering.

My wife produced two or three sheets of paper and handed these to me. She had written patients' names and amounts owed, a fairly extensive list.

She said, "Potter left before collecting all the monies owed him, so you can claim those."

That was the first good news since I took over Potter's practice. I nodded, folded the sheets and put these in my coat pocket. I tried to appear business-like and appreciative, but probably unconvincingly.

But Maud wasn't through. She continued, "David, you have been too easy, letting some patients off without paying. We simply cannot afford charity on such a scale. You are too soft, David."

No question this time: she viewed me with condescension if not contempt, and I became angry. I began to retort, then forced my mouth closed, tried to calm myself, finally saying, "The major problem is that Potter absconded immediately after I gave him the cheque, leaving me to pick up everything on my own, on the run. He is the problem, not me."

My wife also composed her features, telling me, "I was offered a job, keeping the books of the Landrum estate. The man who was doing this has turned senile, has let things get completely out of hand, and the solicitor who handles legal matters for them has asked me to take over."

This caught me in the pit of my stomach. A host of questions filled my mind. I tried to sort through these, finally beginning with, "How did you know of this situation?"

Maud replied, somewhat evasively I thought, "I talked to the solicitor."

Silence while I formulated my next question. "Just on the chance or did Peter Landrum tell you about the situation?"

Maud flushed, finally saying, "David, I am not your servant. I am your equal, and will not let you cross-examine me as though I were on trial. Understand that."

We looked at each other. I could hardly credit what I was hearing. After a moment, I glanced toward the kitchen. The housekeeper-cook had retreated there and closed the door.

I simply couldn't think of anything to say, anything that wouldn't cause a major eruption. Maud's shifting the conversation by introducing women's rights was clever of her, I had to admit. I needed to reformulate my questions, but I was just too tired, and too angry, to think clearly. I stood up, wiped my mouth with my napkin, threw it on the table, turned and walked away, up the stairs to our bedroom.

There, I put on pyjamas and went to the bathroom to clean my teeth, another thing Maud had gotten me to do, then I went to our bed and lay down. I hoped for sleep, for unconsciousness. I needed to escape from the state of my marriage, but tossed, thinking of things I could have said, should have said. At some point, Maud came to bed also, but as far as emotional distance, might as well have stayed in London.

Walking to my surgery the next morning, I realized that in a sense Maud was right. I was in a business and had to pay attention to that. I wasn't in the Army anymore, paid by the Crown. It occurred to me that a partial solution to the problem, for I was still reluctant to ask my patients directly for money, was to have the nurse collect the fees. That would take care of the day to day remunerations, leaving the arrears. I would have to deal with those, I guessed, and I shrank from that.

But this issue left me additionally annoyed with my wife, with her bullying. I remembered Maud's mother remarking that Maud had increased profits. Did she do this by bullying her father? But my main concern was of course with her affections, her faithfulness.

The next day it turned cool, and when I returned I was hoping for a good coal fire, but here again I was balked. Maud insisted we had to keep our costs down, so was rationing the fire as well as, I reflected, her favours. We ate in absolute silence after that, silence broken by the housekeeper-cook, who had purchased some things for our meals. I had to reimburse her from the monies in the jar. Maud, perhaps trying to be conciliatory, offered to convert the growing collection of coins to banknotes. I nodded in acceptance.

The coolness continued, within as well as without the cottage, in every sense. My wife and I were now fairly estranged, and I simply didn't know what to say or do. I was by this time convinced she either was seeing or had been seeing Landrum, certainly was planning to see him in the future. I was a cuckold, that age-old figure of fun. At times, I became so angry I could hardly do my job.

One of the groundskeepers on the Landrum estate had a bad slash on his arm from a scythe. He was keeping the grass about the manor in check, a regular task, but because the injury looked serious, he was brought to me in a motor by the head groundskeeper. It was a long, deep slash, but no tendons were cut, no artery opened. Still it required stitching. I cleaned the wound first, and then sewed it up. The nurse-receptionist was on an errand. The head groundskeeper found some excuse to go to a pub, as he didn't care to watch. So the injured man and I were alone for a while.

I took the opportunity to ask him, "Is Peter Landrum in residence?"

The man raised his eyebrows at my lack of attention to Landrum's title, but answered, "Comes down now and then, mostly lives in London."

I tied off a stitch, asked, "Are his parents in residence?"

Another look of disapproval, but finally the man said, "Earl and Countess mostly stay abroad. France, Spain." Silence, then he went on, "Hear they never got over the death of the older son in South Africa. Boer War. He was favourite. Didn't care much for Lord Peter. Sad in a way."

I began bandaging the man's arm.

I said, "I knew him in school."

The man, now more forthcoming, said, "So you know the story, then."

I replied, "We were in different houses, but everyone knew the story. I felt sorry for the boy and for his parents."

One last bandage, and the man commented, "Parents did all right out of it, money changed hands, so I heard."

So the rumour was true, or at least was widely believed.

I asked, "Any daughters?"

The man, now on his feet, nodded. "One. Married. Lives in Essex. Has two sons, next heirs."

The head groundskeeper was back and I presented him with his repaired subordinate, telling them to return in a week, or sooner if the man became feverish. I didn't think there would be any problems, but had to be certain they understood what to do, if there were any. Eventually the nurse-receptionist and I were able to leave. As I walked to my cottage, I thought about what I had heard. I was relieved Landrum was away; but of course when he returned, he and my wife could do what they wished with little reference to me. While in London, Maud had to keep what she was doing concealed from her parents. Whatever they had known about Landrum's attentions before Maud and I married, I couldn't imagine them joining in such a conspiracy against me. Nor would her brother, I thought.

In a way, I almost felt sorry for Peter Landrum. His parents probably tolerated him rather than loved him. Or perhaps his behaviour had alienated them, disappointed them too often. His failure to marry—what was that about, I wondered—had added to their unhappiness with their heir.

Home once again to a meagre fire, a cold house and a cold wife. Though looking at her across the table, she seemed nervous, apprehensive. I kept a grim silence while I ate. Finished with the meal, I folded my arms on the table after the housekeeper-cook removed our plates. Once again, she closed the door to the kitchen.

Finally, Maud began to speak: "David, I apologize. Your questioning angered me and I angered you in turn. You know my feelings about how women are treated, and that set me off."

I had been thinking about what I was going to say. I still dreaded asking the ultimate question, "Are you sleeping with Peter Landrum?", but I felt I needed to assert myself.

So I told my wife, "If you are my equal, then I am yours. As your husband, no as your spouse, I have a right, a right to know what is going on. I have a right to know if your affections are divided, if my trust in you is justified or not."

I fancied she looked relieved, as once again, I had evaded the key issue.

She replied, "You can trust me, David, to work in your best interest. There is no division between us on that score. I will support you faithfully as far as making a living, keeping your house, comforting you as a wife should."

Hearing this, my feelings sank from despondence toward desolation. She was not going to answer, which in itself was an answer. My feelings must have appeared on my face, as her expression shifted, from near triumph, through concern to a hint of sympathy. I folded my napkin and set it next to my plate.

I rose and she said, "David, you look tired, and you have rounds tomorrow, don't you?"

I nodded. Tomorrow morning was visiting patients in the near parish. Without another word, I mounted the stairs, undressed in our bedroom, donned pyjamas and a dressing gown and cleaned my teeth in our bathroom. Then I climbed into bed, still wearing the dressing gown, as it was cold.

Despite being tired, I once again found it hard to sleep. At some point, Maud joined me in the bed. I tried not to toss and turn, but frequently got up and went into the bathroom to empty what had collected in my bladder. The night advanced, a few minutes each time I looked.

22

DEAD MAN'S CROFT

It was still dark when I finally decided to start my day. After bathroom duties I dressed and went downstairs. I was going to toast some bread and eat that with jam and butter before setting out, as I would need something. However, the housekeeper-cook must have heard me and appeared wearing a dressing gown and slippers. Bless her kind soul, she insisted on fixing some bacon and eggs. And today was actually her day off. I ate, thanked her sincerely, picked up my medical bag and went out.

There was some light coming from the east which grew as I walked. The air was misty, everything wet, the landscape mysterious, long-shadowed. I tried to walk briskly but my legs were leaden. I wondered if I was coming down with something. I was in the lane next the dry stone wall below the "good man's croft" and my ancestral home. I remembered Maud's insistence I stay away, but was feeling rebellious. So I decided to climb the rise and stand on my home site. I wasn't sure what I was hoping for; comfort, perspective, some distancing from my troubles.

So I set my medical bag across the wall, against it to hide it from passers-by. I climbed over the wall and began walking toward the high meadow next the "good man's croft." The sheep readily parted for me. The "good man's croft" was even more sinister looking, a hairy wart on the landscape. No birds again. This suddenly struck me as strange. Looking about, I could see birds in trees elsewhere.

As I crossed the edge of the rocky soil defining the end of the high meadow, I thought I heard a muffled moan, just at the fringe of my hearing. At that point, I was caught by a sneeze, an explosive one, blowing mucus over my face and lapels. I cursed, "Bugger", struggled for a handkerchief and sneezed again.

I at length extracted the handkerchief, still cursing, mopped my face and the front of my clothes. I finally folded the now sodden handkerchief and stuffed it into a side pocket. Then something, some sound, a hint of movement at the corner of my eye, made me turn. Peter Landrum, a desperate expression on his face, was swinging a shovel at my head!

I put up my left arm and ducked my head. The blade of the shovel was raised some by hitting my arm, so the flat of the shovel blade hit the side of my face. Stars, I was nearly knocked over but managed to grab the shovel handle. The two of us struggled for possession, and then Landrum tried to kick me in the groin.

My experience playing against him at school made me anticipate this, and I turned just enough so his kick hit my left thigh, turning me but I managed to keep hold of the shovel. I lunged, driving him backward, and his heel encountered one of the rocks, part of the foundation of my ancestors' dwelling.

He staggered, managed to right himself but lost his grip on the shovel. I in turn staggered backward when he released it, but I was able to wrench the shovel away from him. I half-turned, throwing the shovel as far away as I could to disarm Landrum, a mistake as he recovered his footing and sprang at me, his face a picture of rage and his hands around my throat. He was trying to throttle me. I was driven back; I tripped on something, a rock, and went down, Landrum on me. My left side hit one of the stones of the circle. I felt my ribs crack and Landrum was choking me. My right arm hit another rock, one of the big ones I had dug up as a boy. I tore it loose, it was long and pointed and I swung it at his head.

The pointed end hit the side of his head. I swung the rock again and again, felt his hands loosen, saw blood on the side of his head and swung the rock once, twice, three times more. I saw his eyes unfocus but he was now lying atop me and I dropped the rock and began trying to push him off.

He was a dead weight and I was injured, and my struggles to free myself were not helping my condition. I pushed, levered, managed to draw one leg up then used it to help push him off. He fell to his side and lay on his back, his arms and legs flopping loosely. I rose painfully and looked at his face; his eyes were set, fixed, and I had seen enough men die that I knew he had gone. I had killed him, killed my rival, killed him on his family's land, killed him while I was trespassing.

To me it was a clear case of self-defence, but his family, whatever their feelings for him, would want me to pay for what I had done. I most certainly did not want to hang for the bastard, but how could I prove my innocence?

I stood, breathing heavily still, every breath painful, trying to think what to do. Hide his body in the "good man's croft"? My own injuries were obvious and would raise questions. The "good man's croft": what in Hell was he doing in there? I had to go and see.

I stepped carefully around him lest he was lying doggo, feigning death or unconsciousness, an absurd precaution, but I wasn't taking chances. I tried to follow his traces in the vegetation: the dew was heavy and I could see his track well enough once I focused on it.

It went into the good man's croft. Inside, darkness, fallen limbs, some newly fallen, some rotted, tangled, yet I could see traces of a path. Trees, some huge, clearly very old, kept the growing light to a minimum. The path skirted trees and limbs, though I had to climb over some limbs. Once more I heard moaning, now distinct, and another sound: a horse's whinny. I guessed Landrum's bay was tied up somewhere.

An enormous yew tree, at least 30 feet across, blocked my way. I remembered hearing the yew was considered a sacred tree by some, perhaps the Celts, and this one was very, very old. Landrum's trail went around it, and I followed, still looking back now and then to see if he was following me.

I skirted the yew and on the far side, still in deepest shadow I saw where the moaning was coming from: a small white figure stretched out atop a great boulder. As my eyesight adjusted to the darkness, more details appeared: the boulder was shaped like a horse's hoof, only upside down, so its top surface was flat yet tilted. The figure was a boy, naked, with his arms pulled out, held by heavy thongs. His legs were also secured, spread apart. His mouth had what I guessed was surgical tape across it, so moaning was all the sound he could make.

I saw his eyes turn toward me. We stared at each other, and then I said, "Here, let me help."

I pulled the tape off his face. He said, "Ow. 't hurts!"

I replied, "Yes, it always does, but it has to come off. Let me try to free you."

I searched for my folding pocket knife, bent down to look at the boy's bottom and saw blood around his anus; he had been ruthlessly sodomized. I cut away at the thongs or straps holding the boy. This was slow work, for they were leather, very heavy. One hand released. I cut the other hand strap eventually, and the boy slid back, his feet now on the ground. This loosened the foot straps just enough. I could pull back on the loops so his feet came free.

Freed, he looked tearfully at me, and I tried to be encouraging. "I will try to get a surgeon to put you right. It will hurt, but you should recover."

I looked around, saw a small heap of clothing near another tree and saw something else: a camera. I remembered seeing Landrum with one and hearing he developed pictures. I thought I could guess what the pictures showed. I told the boy, who was starting to shiver, "Put your clothes on and let us leave this place."

He began dressing. He moved stiffly, not liking to bend over, so I had to reach down for his shirt and trousers. No drawers, no stockings either, just shoes which I had to help him tie. I guessed he was one of the poor children Landrum was credited with helping.

The boy kept looking about, and then asked me, "He be back?"

East End, I thought, the depths of the slums. I replied, "No. Landrum is dead. He attacked me and we fought and I killed him."

"Cor," said the boy. He did not seem displeased.

We "wended our way" through, around, over, sometimes under tangled vegetation. This was an awkward process, painful to us both. I had to lift the boy over some downed limbs. He seemed awestruck by the thickness of the growth, well so was I. I could easily believe this patch had never been farmed.

Closer to open country: dawn. The sunlight was very cheering, and I was aching, sore, stumbling. Every breath hurt, but I wasn't coughing blood. I had cracked ribs, which should heal. Sooner or later. The boy looked at me carefully for the first time and commented on my bruised face.

I asked him, "What is your name?"

"Tommy, Tommy Tinker."

"Your parents will be very happy to have you back, I am sure."

Silence as we cleared the last of the "good man's croft," and then Tommy said, "Don't know me pa. Ma's a 'ore. Sends me out when she's fuckin' a customer."

I digested this, and then said, "I am still sure she is probably worried about you."

The boy looked doubtful, but now we were approaching Landrum's body. On his back, he still looked the essence of nobility: strikingly handsome, unobtrusively though obviously expensively dressed. As I looked, flies began to settle on his open, fixed eyes and around his slightly parted lips. I guessed the birds that lived in the "good man's croft," that Landrum's activities had scared away, would soon return to peck at his eyes. Plenty of carrion now. Closed coffin, I thought.

Tommy however was not impressed at all. "Bastard," he said and spit on Landrum's corpse. Tommy added some expressions I thought were confined to soldiers, and then used only *in extremis.*

We started down the slope. I warned Tommy not to step in the dung piles as they might still be slippery and neither of us could afford a fall. I thought of taking the boy's hand but guessed that was what Landrum had done, so told the boy, "you can steady yourself holding onto my coat." We were approaching some clusters of sheep, from which the boy shrank. "They are only sheep." I said reassuringly.

Despite my assurances, Tommy stayed very close trying to keep me between him and the sheep. At length, he took my hand, so I guessed he had decided I was trustworthy.

He asked me, "Wot's yer name?"

I replied as we moved around three or four sheep, "My name is Mendy, David Mendy. I am a doctor."

"Cor."

"Tommy, the police are going to have to be told about all this."

Tommy shook his head, "Don't want nuffin to do with 'leece."

"Tommy, you must tell the police what happened, everything, or I might be charged with Landrum's murder. That could mean I would hang. Will you tell the police everything, be completely honest, leaving nothing out, if only for my sake?"

I looked at him. He looked up at me and he finally said, "Awright."

Close to the dry stone wall now. I looked to my right and could see my medical bag still next the wall. I would have to leave it there; right now I had to figure out how the two of us could get over the wall. I knew I hadn't the strength to carry the bag as well as myself, even without having to help Tommy. At the wall I leaned against it, resting my arms on its top.

I thought then told Tommy, "I will try to lift you to stand on the top of the wall. Then I will try to cross it myself, then lift you down the other side. All right?"

Tommy nodded, and I put my hands under his arms and lifted. Tommy was light, but I thought I would drop him, the pain in my side and other places was so intense, yet I managed to set him upright on top of the wall. Now to get myself over. After a minute or so, breathing and sweating, searching for hand and toe holds in the rock. I stepped up on a toe hold with my relatively unbruised right leg and grasped the wall with both hands. I swung my left leg, most stiff and painful, on the top of the wall and pulled myself up and rolled over to drop on my right leg. I was over. Lifting Tommy and setting him down on the lane side of the wall was much easier.

There was a village perhaps a mile further along the lane. More to the point, a constable resided in the village. Even more to the point, he had a telephone. I told Tommy this as we walked down the lane. He still seemed reluctant.

"Just tell them the truth: don't invent anything or leave anything out. You have done nothing wrong, you are a victim. And it could save my life."

At this he again assented, much more decisively, which reassured me.

I added, as we slowly moved toward our destination, "And I meant it, the part about getting you to a surgeon to sew you up. After a few days, you should be right as rain and have quite a story to tell your friends." He seemed cheered by this and took my hand again.

Glancing down at Tommy, I realized he had black hair. Good features, once cleaned of dirt, short—hard to tell what his age was, perhaps 9 or 10—slight, very like my wife in some respects. A disturbing thought on many levels. Then, something else: I had seen Landrum's fag many times, but only at a distance, half my life ago, but . . . that boy also had, I seemed to recall, black hair. And something more: our school had no formal uniform, unlike some schools, but I vaguely recalled that fags in Landrum's house were supposed to wear grey jackets, perhaps . . . this was at the edge of my memory now, but the jackets had blue trim. Very like the expensive silk dress I had seen Maud wearing the day she had visited me in hospital and when I had returned unexpectedly after I was furloughed. I now understood she was wearing it at Landrum's instance, my arrivals, first when I was wounded and later, had almost certainly interrupted some sort of trysts . . . did Landrum think of her as a replacement, a reminder, of his dead love? I shook my head, regretted doing so and saw the constable's house ahead. I pointed this out to Tommy.

23

QUESTIONS AND ANSWERS

❖

Yet another thought occurred to me and I asked Tommy, "Did Landrum take pictures of you?"

Tommy looked up at me, then evidently remembered his pledge to tell everything, and he told me, "Aye. Took pictures of me starkers, maybe pissing or on the shitter."

This was all starting to make sense, an awful sense and I knew I must, for my own sake, convince the police to have the film in Landrum's camera developed and to search Landrum's dark room. If Landrum was making a photographic record of his activities, he would keep those pictures well locked up.

I couldn't pin Tommy's accent down more precisely than East End. Of course, a boy from the streets was likely to have an indeterminate accent. He continued, "Lud Peter ast me if I wanna see 'is place in the country. He sed 'e would take me in 'is motor. I said, 'sure' an' we started after dark. 'E drove up where I 'uz waitin'. When we gots there, we drives into stables. No one 'round. 'E say, let me clean yer face, an' 'e pours somethin', somethin' 'eavy smellin' on a towel and puts it on me face an' I wakes up, me mouf taped an' 'im bumfuckin' me."

Chloroform, I thought. Ether would be too volatile.

I knocked at the constable's door. And knocked. I heard someone inside, and then the door opened: a woman looking a bit resentful, therefore the constable's wife. She stared at me, realized the situation was serious, and turned to call her husband. Unnecessary as the man himself emerged, towelling his face. He also stared at me.

I said, "I was attacked by Peter Landrum with a shovel. I think he was trying to kill me, afraid I would find out that he was sodomizing this boy, probably before Landrum murdered him. Landrum and I fought and I broke his head with a rock. In self-defence. Landrum is dead. The boy needs the attention of a surgeon, as he is torn up about his . . ." I glanced toward the man's wife, but she was disappearing into the kitchen, hopefully to get us some tea. I finished my statement, ". . . anus."

This was a lot to take in at once. The constable said, "Lord Peter dead?"

I nodded and asked, "May I sit down? And this lad needs to lie down, as it is very painful for him to bend over."

The constable picked Tommy up and laid him carefully on a table. I sat down heavily in a chair next the table and rested my head on my crossed arms. The constable went to the telephone, dialled and began summoning his superiors in Cirencester.

The constable's wife came in with tea and even biscuits. Tommy ate and drank as though he had not done either for a day or more, I guessed. I ate some biscuits and drank two mugs of tea while the constable related what I had told him, related it with admirable accuracy. I finished my second mug, noted my hands were shaky, and then lay my head back down on my arms.

I must have fallen asleep, for it seemed I was almost immediately roused by arrival of a police inspector, a sergeant and two other constables. Tommy, I noticed, had fallen asleep despite his injuries. More tea. Chairs were produced. The inspector and sergeant sat down. The sergeant brought out a notebook and prepared to take notes, reminding me anew I was in a serious situation. I decided to keep my story concise; if the inspector had questions he would ask them.

When I began talking, Tommy woke, grimaced, and said, "Bugger!" Appropriately enough, I thought.

I began, "My name is David Mendy. I am doctor to these two parishes. Today was my day to go on rounds to my patients in this parish. I set out early, before dawn, and was on my way when I passed below the high meadow next an untilled piece of land called the 'good man's croft.' I was told by my great-great-grandfather that our ancestors had lived in the high meadow. On an impulse I decided to visit the place, and walked up there. This was on Landrum property, so I was actually trespassing."

Silence save for the sound of the sergeant scribbling.

I continued, "When I there, I thought I heard a moan, very faint. Then I sneezed twice and cursed. As I was turning to leave, I saw Peter Landrum . . ."

Here I was interrupted by the inspector, "You mean Lord Peter Landrum, I believe?"

I answered, "Yes. I knew him at school, so tend to omit the title."

The inspector seemed to disapprove, but I continued:

"He had a shovel in his hands and swung the shovel at my head. Hard. I managed to duck, but the flat of the blade hit the side of my face, here" I said, pointing to the place. "I grabbed the shovel handle, we struggled . . . ."

Another interruption by the inspector, "Was anything said during all this?"

I replied, "Not a word by either of us. I realized he meant to kill me."

I described the struggle and its result, at which point the inspector stood up and with surprising gentleness pulled aside my cravat and collar and looked at my throat. Then he sat down, telling the sergeant, "Bruising about the throat, consistent with the story."

I felt cheered by this corroboration, but went on, "I again heard a moan, realized it must be coming from the 'good man's croft,' went into the place and found this boy," indicating Tommy. "He was naked, his hands and feet tied apart by heavy leather straps. His mouth was covered by a strip of surgical tape, so all he could do was moan. I saw blood about his . . . rectum, and realized he had been brutally sodomized. I freed him and we were able to walk here to the constable's, who summoned you."

The inspector didn't try to check on Tommy's injury, just asked him, "What is your name, lad?"

Tommy said, "Tommy Tinker."

The inspector, glancing at me, said, "I will talk to him alone. Can you do your rounds now, doctor?"

I looked automatically at my wristwatch, a gift from Maud. The crystal was smashed. I looked up at the wall clock in the constable's parlour, not yet 10. Amazing. I shook my head, shook it slowly, my neck hurt, and replied, "I don't think I am up to doing my rounds. I was lucky to be able to make it to here. If you can drive me back to my surgery, perhaps I can carry on there."

I then remembered, and added, "Tommy here needs the attentions of a surgeon to sew his backside up. Can you see to that?"

The inspector blinked but nodded.

I went on, "Landrum left a camera there. The film should be developed. And I heard he has a darkroom in his family's manor. This I am guessing is kept locked, but he will have carried the key in his pocket. The police should search the darkroom; for, thinking about all this, I strongly suspect you will find pictures of other victims. I believe Landrum has been doing what he was doing to Tommy here for some time. Remember he had a shovel, probably to bury Tommy once he had finished with him. If you search the 'good man's croft,' it is almost certain you will find graves of previous victims."

This was received with stunned silence, and then the sergeant began writing again.

191

I remembered something else and went on, "Landrum's horse is tethered somewhere in the 'good man's croft.' I heard it. There may be evidence in the saddle bags."

Silence, then the inspector asked, "When did this fight occur? Just for our records."

I showed the inspector my watch, which was stopped during the fight. The sergeant noted the time it was stopped and wrote that down.

The inspector turned to one of the constables, who had remained standing during all this, and told the man, "Take Doctor Mendy to his surgery."

I got to my feet, eventually anyway: I had to make two or three attempts first. I turned to Tommy, told him, "Good luck, Tommy."

Tommy replied from his prone position, "Aye, doc. And thanks."

I waved and went outside with one of the constables. A considerable crowd had gathered, drawn by the police visitation. Everyone realized something serious had happened. Everyone also recognized me, noted the bruise on my face, a babble of comment began as I entered the police motor.

I told the constable driving, "Back along the lane. I will show you where Landrum's body is. And I have to recover my medical bag."

We drove in silence; not for long, it was actually a short distance, at least in a motor. At the "good man's croft," I pointed out the place. Many birds gathered now, clustered about Landrum's body. I wondered if Landrum had exposed his dead victims on that boulder for the birds before he buried the remains. The boulder did resemble an altar.

I said, "I found the boy near the middle of that patch of woods, the far side of a great yew."

The constable nodded and we drove a short distance until I remembered my bag and told the constable, "Stop here. I need my medical bag."

He did, I got out and stiffly moved to the dry stone wall. I looked over, saw the bag and went to it. I reached over the wall and pulled it up. It seemed very heavy but everything seemed heavy and slow. Turning, I saw the constable had followed me, I suppose in case I ran for it. I wished I was in a condition to do anything of the sort.

The constable took me to my surgery. I extracted myself from the police motor, thanked him and said, "I will be here unless I collapse. Then I will be at my house."

I went inside. The nurse was there, dealing with routine matters. Also collecting fees, for I had told her to do this. A few patients. Everyone was shocked at my appearance. Looking in the mirror, I was shocked myself: the left side of my face was dark and swollen, I was going to have a very black eye, and my clothes were dishevelled and stained with dirt. There were a few tears in my coat, and I moved like I looked and felt.

My nurse asked me, "You going to see patients, Doctor?"

"I will try. My rounds were interrupted. You will hear all about it shortly. What time is it?"

She checked her watch, said, "Ten-fifteen."

"Send the first patient in."

I was able to deal with three patients. I was slow but they were, well, patient. The fourth patient was one of those who were behind on payments. Maud's list of these had survived my morning's adventures. Perhaps because of my injuries, or perhaps because I had reached my limit, I refused to treat her until she made up the arrears. She was affronted, made as if to leave, but I was adamant. No payment, no treatment, I told her, adding that she could find another doctor if she wouldn't pay her debt to me. (And to Potter, but I didn't say that.) After a glaring contest, she opened her purse and I told her the total: 3/3/2. She blanched at this, I saw tears in her eyes but I remained resolute. She slowly counted out the money, which I pocketed after writing her a receipt.

She required a prescription, which I wrote out after my examination. However, I insisted on a half-crown before handing it to her. I wasn't going to start up another long score. Once more, we were at loggerheads, but she eventually conceded the point, also the half-crown. No feeling of triumph after she left, nor shame either; I was just not going to be taken advantage of any more.

Noon brought an offer by my nurse to get me a sandwich and a pint from the pub, an offer I gratefully accepted. I continued to see patients while she was out, and noticed looks from the recent arrivals indicating that what had happened this morning was known. No problems with collections, perhaps my condition and grim manner were intimidating. I didn't like to play the bully, but if my patients didn't like my demeanour, that was their problem, not mine.

After the lunch, for which I repaid my nurse, I met with the afternoon's patients. Usually there were more in the afternoon. I dealt with two more defaulters in the same way with the same results, clearing two more arrears. Again, no feeling of triumph, just doing what was necessary.

By now, I was certain the story of my encounter with Landrum and its result, together with revelations of his practices were known to all. I wasn't sure how it affected their opinion of me as a doctor, but it certainly made collecting my fees easier. In fact, I was getting the idea that some patients were coming in just to have a look at me.

Late in the afternoon, I was beginning to wilt. Here I had a visitor, two in fact: the chief inspector for the shire constabulary and a sergeant. No constables in attendance, which heartened me; clearly I was not going to be arrested, at least not immediately. I found a second chair for the sergeant and sat heavily down myself. I noticed the sergeant was not taking notes, another good sign.

The chief inspector said, "The boy confirmed your story. We found the camera and are having the film developed. One of the constables thought he found a grave near the stone where the boy was tied. We are still searching."

I interrupted, "How is the boy?"

"We had a surgeon sew him up. The boy is asleep under sedation. The surgeon thinks he will be alright."

"Thank God for that," I said fervently.

The chief inspector raised his eyebrows but continued:

"We found the horse and looked in the saddle bags. From what the boy told us, we suspect Landrum used chloroform on the boy. We found a bottle of the stuff along with some cloths in the saddle bags, also a roll of surgical tape, so that checks out.

"We searched Landrum's body and found some keys. We paid a visit to the manor. Since we are investigating a cause of death, not a possible criminal act, we didn't think we needed a search warrant. The butler showed us where the dark room was, told us only Landrum had keys to the place. We opened it and looked about in the presence of the butler. Two cabinets were locked, but Landrum's keys opened these." The chief inspector paused, and then continued, "Inside were albums for photographs. The photographs were, well . . ."

He had stopped. I could guess at their contents, but asked, "How many victims?"

"At least five. We have contacted Scotland Yard, but they said people, including children, disappeared every week in a city as big as London."

I commented, "The boys would be short, slender, with good features and black hair. That might narrow the search some."

The chief inspector nodded and said, "I will tell Scotland Yard this." Silence before the chief inspector resumed, "There will be an inquest, and you will have to testify."

"Certainly."

The chief inspector then told me, "The butler was horrified, especially at the pictures. He undertook to notify Landrum's parents. He said they were travelling in the Aegean."

What a homecoming, I thought. The press would . . . come to think of it, the press would be after me too. Fame. Now all I needed was Fortune.

The chief inspector and his sergeant left, and I resumed my practice. I should have felt relieved, for myself anyway: I was not going to stand trial for Landrum's murder. Yet all I felt was sadness: Landrum had all the gifts, but was possessed by a Devil. His parents were probably aware of his tendencies in some respects;

perhaps that was why they stayed away, hoping for good news of their son yet fearing scandal. Their fears would be over fulfilled.

Still more patients. With clearing up some more of the arrears, this was going to be a profitable day, a thought that brought Maud to mind. I tried to shake her out of my thoughts, concentrating on the human being before me. At last darkness; my nurse and I could go to our homes. Home. Now I had no defence, no distraction. I said goodnight to the nurse, thanked her for her assistance and turned toward my house.

How would Maud take it? Her lover dead, and at my hands. Would she leave me? I found I really didn't care: she could stay or go as she chose. I would continue. But was Landrum really her lover, her physical lover? Given his preferences, what were his practices? Clearly he was not disposed to marry her. If Maud had wanted a divorce, I would have had to release her. Yet there was no hint of anything of the sort. I stumbled, recovered, and continued walking. This day was beyond overlong and I thought I had passed my limit hours ago yet was still on my feet, still moving.

And what about Maud's bookkeeping job? Presumably she would be sacked, given her connection with me, though perhaps not. I really didn't know enough about the situation in that household, or about Landrum's parents. If she was as valuable to the estate as I guessed she might well be, perhaps she would be kept on.

24

A GOOD COAL FIRE

---◆---

I was at my door. The housekeeper-cook was away, so only Maud and I were there. Now I found I would be able to ask the questions that had troubled me for years and demand full and honest answers. I opened the door. I heard a kind of hiccoughing wail, subdued so I hadn't heard it from outside. An eerie sound, for I had never heard my wife crying.

I paused at the money jar and automatically began transferring banknotes and coins to it. Despite muffling by the banknotes, it made a brave sound. Maud stopped crying and turned toward me. With the few coals alight, it was hard to see, yet I caught reflections of tears on her face. I added the last coins to the jar and moved toward the sofa my wife was sitting on.

Maud's shawl had fallen from her shoulders. And it was a cold evening. Without reflecting, I picked up her shawl and put it back across her shoulders. Then I moved to the fire and began adding more coal. This was strictly contrary to orders, but I needed the heat. Maud stirred but said nothing. At least she had stopped crying.

As I added the coal, I saw some partly charred cloth. As the light grew, I recognized it as the grey silk dress Maud presumably wore to meetings with Landrum. I flicked the rest of it more completely into the fire using the poker, watching the arching blue flame consume it.

I built up the fire. The room brightened, the air warmed. I sat heavily down on the sofa, stretched out my legs and absorbed the heat. Perhaps I would make it to another day. I forced myself to concentrate on the issues between my wife and myself. I turned to Maud:

"I assume you heard. Peter Landrum attacked me with a shovel when he imagined I was going to discover his vile pastime. We fought and I killed him. In self-defence. I rescued his latest victim. The police have accepted my story, but how many other victims of his are buried in the 'good man's croft' aren't known yet."

Maud nodded, "Everyone at the Manor was shocked. Peter was not a favourite but no one suspected . . . . David, I am so sorry. Sorry I hurt you, distressed you. I fell far short of my duties as a wife."

She fell silent, gazing at the fire. The dress, probably including the buttons, was now brittle black ashes. Maud resumed, "He bought the dress for me."

I said, "I dimly recall the fags in Landrum's house, including the one who killed himself, wore grey jackets with blue trim."

Maud bowed her head. I saw fresh tears. She struggled to compose herself. Finally she began to speak again, "David, as a girl growing up, my heroines were Lizzie Hexam, whom we once talked about, Jane Eyre, and Jane Fairfax, Jane Austen's character from *Emma*." I nodded. Maud said, "These were girls with no money who worked hard for education or accomplishments and who as a result were able to marry gentlemen, men with enough money so they didn't have to worry about sixpences.

"But that was the point: having enough money meant the man and woman could devote all their time and love to each other, each was the centre of the other's world. That was what I wanted, not having to share a husband with a job."

I was silent. Maud correctly interpreted my silence, saying, "I did sympathize with your struggles, your efforts to become qualified, but when I met Peter, I thought he was just the man I had always dreamed about." Another pause before she resumed, "I did begin to meet him. Ma and Pa didn't approve, so our meetings had to be in secret. We talked. He told me about the boy, said he would never forgive himself, and that was why he was helping street children. Of course, I never suspected his real motive. Even now . . .

"But Peter also told me about his parents' coldness toward him, how they had favoured his older brother and I felt sorry for him. Then when he went off to fight, I worried and prayed for him. On his leaves he would tell me about snipers and trench raids and hand-to-hand combat and I was so thrilled such a hero seemed to care for me."

This comment set me off. I asked sarcastically, "While I was skulking behind the line in a hole in the ground?" Then I forced myself to be calm, to be analytical. I asked, "Was he ever mentioned in dispatches? You must have been perusing the newspapers."

Maud shook her head, saying, "David, I was just telling you how I felt then. I was fixed on him, and dismissed and undervalued you. No, he never was, unlike you."

I asked, "Was he ever wounded? Decorated? Was he promoted above captain?"

Maud again shook her head, sighed, and told me, "No. On all counts. The only time his name was printed in the papers was when he was made ADC to some general. This was to help with recruiting. It was before the Armistice. You were still serving, still in danger; and, God forgive me, the only thing I felt was joy at his being out of danger. And those stories he told me, that I assumed involved him, may have happened, may have happened to other men or perhaps were invented. I just don't know."

I felt I had to be just toward him, "He served through several years of that shambles, so he must be counted a brave man and honoured if for that alone."

Maud turned toward me and said, "Thank you for that, David. At least I married the one decent man in my life."

I couldn't avoid the central issue any more. I asked, "Were you unfaithful to me with that creature?"

A pause. Maud was staring into the fire. Finally, she replied, "In a sense yes, in another sense, no. Let me try to explain. I was, and am, fond—very fond of you, David. When we were together, when you were on leave, perhaps I was more than fond. I kept telling myself, and my parents told me, I was lucky to have you. You are a very good husband, your achievements are very impressive and you loved me very much. I was happy when I was with you.

"But with Peter I was in another world, a world of romance, a fairy tale world. I loved him so much; I would do anything for him. When we were alone together, it was as though no one else existed, just the two of us."

As she said this, I remembered a conversation I had with her early in our courtship. For the first time I understood that my wife whom I had always taken to be practical, matter-of-fact, and controlled was actually intensely, wildly romantic. She did like me to do romantic things for her, but I was irredeemably from her world, her lower middle-class, striving world, a world of limits and boundaries. That was driven home to her over and over again, during our courtship. So she was in fact really reluctant to marry me as this meant abandoning a dream. Whether this realization earlier would have made any difference to our marriage was beyond my ability to say.

Maud swallowed, hesitated, and then resumed. "We did have sex of a sort together. He told me he didn't want to chance getting me with child, so . . ." Here she stopped, then forced herself to continue, ". . . he used me from . . . from behind . . . in my bottom. It was uncomfortable but" another hesitation before, "he used his finger to satisfy me. Sometimes I would . . ." Here she nerved herself to speak, ". . . satisfy him in other ways. He told me he couldn't marry me, his parents would disinherit him, but I didn't care. So in a sense I committed adultery with him and in a sense I didn't. But I would have if he had asked me to. I am sorry, David. I know this bothered you, but I couldn't bring myself to confess what I had done and was doing. I couldn't help myself. To me, he was like a god."

"He was a monster," I said, then remembered some of the stories from Greek mythology. In a sense, both our statements were true, but I didn't want to go further into the theology.

"David, I just wanted to be part of his life, a comforting part, allowing him to escape his sorrows and be happy. I thought we were sharing something precious, so precious no one else mattered, and I was proud to be his . . . mistress, concubine, companion, or whatever you want to call it. Now, now what were enchanted moments together are moments of . . . of degradation, times I will always be ashamed of.

"I always thought of myself as a clever woman. He fooled me because I wanted to be fooled, I wanted to believe completely in him, and I did so and I deserve my humiliation." Silence again. My wife resumed, "I am so ashamed, David. I thought he loved me."

I replied, "I think you were actually a substitute for the boy I told you about; the boy who killed himself rather than continue to be used by Landrum. Perhaps Landrum also wanted to see if he could have some sort of sexual relationship with a woman." I twisted slightly to try to ease some bruised muscles. This was not very successful. I thought of another possible reason he had seduced her and said, "Did he ask you to spy on me?"

Maud was silent a moment, "Not exactly. He was very concerned about your trespassing and solicited my help in keeping you away from that place. I did ask you to promise to stay clear of it. But I cannot complain about a broken promise, considering my behaviour. David, I had no idea, yet it is now clear what was going on. But it is so hard to believe.

"When I told Peter what had happened, that we had quarrelled and you had gone to Gloucestershire, he urged me to follow you. Perhaps that was his motive. I don't know. He did tell me about his estate needing a bookkeeper and said we could still meet there. So you guessed right about the situation.

"My brother and his wife visited a day or so after you left. He told me he liked you, thought I was lucky to have you as a husband, and I should follow you. Ma and Pa agreed. Ma said she would do the bookkeeping with a girl who was helping us, and I needn't worry about that.

"I was critical of you over money. You needed encouragement, comforting, and I added to your burdens. I shouldn't have done that either, David. Again I apologize."

I stretched my legs, still quite painful, but the heat of the fire was helping. I asked, "Did he take pictures of you?"

Maud was again silent before saying, "He wanted to. From behind. He said it was artistic. I didn't want to and he didn't insist. That is the only time I refused him something." A pause, then, "But it was a near thing, because if he had insisted, I would have done that, too."

I remarked, "If you hadn't refused, any pictures of you would now be part of the police file on Landrum."

A long silence this time before she said, "It would have been no more than I deserve, David."

I could see more tears in her eyes and I heard the break in her voice. I decided I had reproached her enough. Perhaps the influence of the warm fire.

Maud continued, "But the worst thing of all is how I treated you, how I hurt you, and you deserved nothing of the sort. I can never forgive myself for my treatment of you, David."

We were both looking into the fire during this conversation. I was actually not surprised by what Maud told me; indeed the reality was somewhat short of my fears and imaginings. In a sense, I had been freed from the incubus of Peter Landrum, freed from my emotional servitude to my wife. So in a sense was she freed from emotional servitude to Peter Landrum. And I was in my home. I would recover from my injuries.

"David, have you eaten?" my wife asked, her head turned toward me. I turned toward her and for the first time she saw my bruised face. "Oh David, your face!" and she raised her hand to gently touch my face. And I in turn raised my right hand and caressed hers, brushing away a few tears as I did so.